A Golden Weekend

Larry Carello

For Gary,
Best wishes to a
teammate + friend

Larry

Contact the publisher at:
P. O. Box B
Lakeland, MI 48143

ISBN: 978-0-9802284-0-3

Cover and interior design and layout by Lee Lewis Walsh,
Words Plus Design, www.wordsplusdesign.com

Printed in the United States of America

For my wife

Chapter One

This was the part of the day that the boys hated most. It was bad enough that the weather was cold and windy — February in Upstate New York when people ask themselves if winter will ever end — but on top of that was the wet factor. Dickie and Donny tried desperately but could never steady the big trash can full of water enough to avoid getting soaked. As they sat in the bed of the old pickup truck, it felt as if they were driving all the way to Buffalo and not the mile and a half to work. Their father, Mel, did his best to keep a steady hand on the wheel, but it didn't matter. The water just kept sloshing out.

"Do you think he'll ever buy a new one with a lid?" asked Dickie.

"I doubt it," replied his older brother.

The green plastic can had been around since the boys could remember and its sole function on the planet was to transport water from their home to the family's business to make coffee and orange drink. Dickie and Donny went along with the program obligingly, though, because they knew Mel would reward them with a five dollar bill at the end of the work day. If they were lucky, the eatery would take in thirty to forty dollars today selling hot dogs, hamburgers, and fries to the Sunday drivers making their way to Indian Lake. Money garnered today would serve as the family's main source of income for the week, then next Sunday the trash can would be filled again and off they would go.

Despite the temperature, the lake still attracted visitors, providing an abundant source of entertainment. Ice fishermen huddled over tip-ups and people skated on hand shoveled rinks. During exceptionally cold winters when the ice reached an extra thickness, amateur stock car racers would pool together, plow off a large oval track and ply their skills slipping, sliding and crashing their jalopies into snow banks. Man's natural attraction to water could not be deterred. In liquid state or frozen, the lake was still a magnet.

As they drove slowly down the narrow road, Donny marveled at the depth of the snow. The wind had formed drifts up over the windows of the unoccupied cottages that lined the shore. It was hard to visualize this stark, barren scene in the summer when it came alive with campers and fun seekers. Right now it looked more like the pictures of Siberia Donny had seen in a *National Geographic* magazine at school. The miracle of spring, however, was just a month or so away. Then the metamorphosis would start, slowly at first, but with undeniable force, the ice covering the lake would begin to break up. Wind would propel massive chunks onto the shore as nature's power transformed the frozen plain into an ever-moving body of water.

Mel drove cautiously, not only to help the boys steady the water bucket, but also because the road was covered in ice. A strong west wind pounded the right side of the vehicle causing its rear end to skid and weathervane to the left if he went too fast. Looking in the rear view mirror he saw his two sons, their soaked gloves clamped firmly on the rim of the bucket.

"You guys all right?" Mel hollered out the window to the boys.

"Yeah," they answered in unison. "Just get us there, Dad," Dickie said.

Although their cold journey would last less than ten minutes, Mel knew how miserable this task was for the kids. He never turned on the truck's heater for himself, with the boys sitting in back freezing.

About halfway down Park Avenue they passed Jimmy's Shoreline Inn. The big white-sided building sat empty and dark, its parking lot unplowed. A sign declaring "Closed for Vacation" was taped to a window. The Shoreline's owner, Mel's brother, Jimmy Rosco, and his wife Diane made their pilgrimage to Florida at this time every year. Mel had never been to Florida; in fact the farthest south he had ever traveled was to Central Pennsylvania to visit his aunt. He caught himself daydreaming about how nice it would feel with warm sunshine on his skin instead of the cold drafts that squeezed through the crevices of the truck's doors and windows. Mel checked on the boys again and saw their parkas and hats covered in snow spray. They were laughing about something.

One hundred yards from the building, its faded sign's letters became visible through the blowing snow: Rosco's Fry Shack. Over time, the small concession stand had gathered a loyal following of customers who craved its old style French fried potatoes. Locals referred to it simply as the Shack.

Mel eased the truck into a spot by the building where the snow wasn't so deep, yanked the parking brake lever, and braced himself for wind's onslaught.

"OK, guys, let's go!" Dickie and Donny weren't strong enough to move the can of water themselves so their dad stepped in to help. For a little man, he always amazed the boys with his strength.

"One, two, three, now!" he ordered. Together, the boys nearly equaled their father's muscle as they balanced the weight and lifted the can from the truck's tailgate. Once on the ground it was easier to move as they slid it across the snow and ice surrounding the Shack.

"Donny, once we get things cooking, take the shovel and ice spud to clear a path so no one falls on their ass, will ya?" Mel asked.

"OK, Dad," Donny answered.

It was always a relief when the weather warmed, sometime in April, and the Shack's water could be turned on without fear of pipes bursting. That signaled that the green plastic can could be stowed back in the garage for another year. April, however, was still a long two months away.

Mel unlocked the building's back door and turned on the lights. The air felt a little warmer once the three of them were inside and protected from the wind. The Shack had been built over fifty years ago. It had changed hands a few times but was always used for the same business: selling greasy food, ice cream, and other carnival chow. In years to come this stuff would be referred to as "junk food," but in the 1960s it was not such a sin to eat and everyone enjoyed it.

"Do you think you can mix the orange drink and get it right this time, Donny?" asked Mel.

"Yeah, I think so," he replied. Last week Donny had lost his concentration and screwed up the mixture so badly that their first customer spit it out on the sidewalk, where the liquid promptly froze solid. As they unloaded the truck today Donny noticed that the orange blob of ice hadn't moved. "Four to one water to syrup, right?" Donny asked sheepishly.

"That's right," his dad answered, not looking up as he bent over to light the hot dog grill. Dickie had already turned on the deep fryers and was brewing a pot of coffee. The aroma of heating peanut oil and fresh-brewed java filled the small space and continued to warm the air a little.

The Shack was a two-story, rectangular-shaped building, sixteen by twenty feet in dimension. Built of fir framing and rough-cut knotty pine, it was strictly a fair weather structure, never intended for use in the winter. Removable plywood shutters surrounded its exterior on three sides. In the summer, with all the shutters removed, there was usually a nice breeze coming in from the lake. Today, however, Mel chose to operate in "two shutter mode," exposing only a small area by the fryers and grill on the east end of the building, downwind. Nothing but a snow covered parking lot stood between the Shack and the lake, allowing the west wind to travel unimpeded for over twenty miles across the frozen surface before striking the building.

Mel unlatched the first of the two big shutters, ducking his head to lessen the sting of snow pellets against his face. By combining strength, crude aerodynamics and timing, he successfully maneuvered the shutters off and anchored them in a snow bank next to the building. The fryers were hot and the grills were ready for cooking as Mel stomped the snow off his boots and walked back inside.

Donny finished pouring syrup into the drink machine. The contraption reminded him of a spaceman's helmet like the ones he saw in the movies, its large glass globe perched at eye level. Satisfied that the blend was right, he turned on the machine and watched the orange concoction squirt out from a rotating sprayer inside the globe. In a few minutes the beverage would be mixed and ready to serve.

"Where is everybody?" Dickie whispered to his brother.

"I don't know, probably just getting out of church," said Donny as he tied on his apron. Mel carried a bag of potatoes in from the truck as the boys hovered over the grills struggling to stay warm.

The time was 12:15 p.m. on a February Sunday and the Rosco family was ready for business.

Chapter Two

"Jimmy, where the hell is my Coppertone?" Diane Rosco shouted. Jimmy looked at his watch. It was only 10:30. His wife was up earlier than normal and anxious to get a prime spot on the beach for sunbathing. The three weeks she and Jimmy were spending in Florida came as a welcome relief from the New York State winter. With only a couple days of vacation left, Diane was determined to catch every available sun ray and go back home as tanned as possible.

"I think you left it in the car yesterday," answered her husband. Diane was tearing up a pile of unfolded laundry with the determination of a hungry cat pawing through a leaf pile after a mouse. Jimmy took it all in stride. He was accustomed to helping her find lost items after a drinking binge and last night was one to remember. Diane had slammed down seven drinks at the tiki bar and passed out on the ride back to the motel. During the drive, Jimmy had prayed that there wouldn't be hell to pay in the morning as there usually was with his wife. His marriage to Diane could be described in one word: stormy. Even when sober, Diane was a handful and he didn't have the patience to ride the emotional roller coaster with her today.

Just take your bag full of junk and get the hell out of here, Jimmy thought. Once she was out the door, he planned to spend the day drifting around Daytona Beach checking out activity at the various businesses along highway A1A. Diane could fry on the sand for all he cared. Jimmy never could relax enough to sit idly sunbathing. Sure, he might read a book or newspaper, but that didn't interest him much either. He would rather occupy himself looking for new entrees to expand the menu at his restaurant up north. There was a new place a half hour up the highway that he wanted to try for lunch. A hotel desk clerk had told him they served a delicious Hawaiian style chicken plate and he was eager to go out and sample the meal for himself.

"Have a good day, Diane," Jimmy said as he grabbed his car keys off the dresser. Diane was already heading out the door with an over-stuffed beach bag slung over her shoulder. After locating another bottle of lotion in her makeup case, she had calmed down a bit.

"See you at happy hour," she mumbled. An unfiltered cigarette hung from her chapped lips.

Jimmy Rosco had married Diane Draper shortly after returning from his service in the Navy. Oh, they had some good times during their early years together and she was an adequate mother to their son Freddy. For the last several years, however, her constant whining about not having enough money was wearing him down. *What the hell does she want, anyways?* he wondered. He ran the best restaurant within twenty miles of Woodland Beach and it was rare when she didn't get what she wanted — a new Cadillac every two years, the nicest clothes and even a maid. *Lucky for her I'm a workaholic and not like Mel,* Jimmy thought. *How could Mel's wife Rita stand living with that guy?* Mel barely got by financially but somehow everyone in his family always seemed happy. They all volunteered to work at the Shack during the summer season and never complained. Getting

Diane and his son Freddy to show an ounce of interest in his business was like pulling teeth. It didn't really matter though. Jimmy Rosco had concluded a long time ago that the harder he worked, the more money he would earn and that would be his ticket to happiness. Although, so far in his life, this plan wasn't working so well.

As he drove his El Dorado out the hotel parking lot, Jimmy glanced toward the ocean and saw Diane strutting down the sidewalk on her way to the shore. He shook his head at the sight of her bronzed, rail-thin body wrapped in a short white robe. By now a long stretch of ash hung on the end of her cigarette. Jimmy turned on the car radio and searched for the news.

"Good morning, Mrs. Rosco!" chimed the cabana boy. The day Diane and Jimmy had arrived, she had tipped the kid five bucks. Now, two and a half weeks later, he still charged up to meet her and offer his services. She never bothered to learn his name and simply grunted, "Hi, how are ya," not really caring to hear his answer.

"Front row, close to the water OK?" the young Cuban asked.

"Yup, the usual," she answered. Diane followed him to a long wooden chaise lounge. The boy took a towel from his shoulder and dusted some sand from the chair. She handed him a dollar, he thanked her and ran back to his station to greet the next hotel guest.

For the next six hours Diane would bake in the sun reading a romance novel while her husband cruised A1A.

"Freddy, please stop playing those drums and come to dinner!" begged Rosa. God, how she wished this week would be over. Babysitting her fourteen-year-old grandson was too much for her this year. Freddy was an obnoxious kid used to always getting his way. Jimmy and Diane showered him with every gadget, toy, and gizmo, and the drum set they had given him for Christmas had proven to be one of his favorite diversions. In fact, Rosa was surprised he was still interested in playing and hadn't tossed it aside like he normally did when bored with a new gift. He'd been banging on his drums constantly since getting home from school.

"Take it easy, Grandma, I'll be there when I'm ready," Freddy yelled back.

Freddy had dropped his books on the kitchen table and immediately sat down to an after-school snack. With his grandmother in the living room watching television, he was able to sneak a huge slice from a coconut cream pie, chasing it down with a tall glass of milk. Sated, at least for the time being, Freddy had retreated to his room to practice the drum solo from the surfing song "Wipeout." He was proud of himself for nearly mastering the twenty-second riff over the last couple weeks. After an hour and a half of playing drums and then watching cartoons, Rosa called him to dinner. He ignored her for a moment, then his grandmother called him again, this time baiting the hook to more effectively make her point.

"Freddy, I cooked that pasta and sausage dish you like so much," she pleaded.

"OK, I'll be right there," he answered. The mere mention of pasta or sausage always made his mouth water.

His schoolmates had christened him Fat Freddy when he was in the third grade. That nickname infuriated him and, seeing his reaction, naturally everyone just kept it up. The more angry Freddy got, the more ammo his schoolmates found to torment him.

Rosa wondered how the boys she had raised could have such different lives and such opposite families. Jimmy and Diane craved all the material things that life had to offer, while Mel and

Rita seemed content to just get by. And their children were vastly different as well. Mel's oldest child Sylvia could be a handful with her boy-craziness; the young boys had started lining up for her attention before she was twelve. Rosa prayed that the young beauty, now sixteen, would at least make it through high school before getting pregnant. The girl was gorgeous and she knew it. But despite her flirtatiousness, you could not help but love her, thought Rosa. She was kind and friendly, just like Mel's boys Donny and Dickie. Freddy, on the other hand, was a royal pain in the ass.

"Would you like some milk with your dinner?" Rosa asked.

"Only if you put some chocolate syrup in the glass, too," demanded Freddy. "When are Mom and Dad getting back from Florida?" Spaghetti sauce dripped down from both corners of his mouth.

"Friday night, Freddy. Two more days," Rosa answered.

"Great!" Freddy sat up straighter in his chair and smiled. "Dad promised he would take me shopping for a mini bike when he got back." Rosa visualized this rotund, two hundred and fifteen pound kid scooting around on a small motorized bike. It reminded her of something she'd seen at the circus as a kid when the clowns would ride around the tent on tiny trikes. She chuckled to herself and asked the Lord's forgiveness for privately making fun of her own grandson. She hoped that Freddy would find direction and purpose in his life and every night she said a prayer for him. In the meantime, though, he seemed content to just eat, sleep, and play with all the junk his parents bestowed upon him.

It was an annual ritual for Rosa to babysit Freddy when his parents closed down their restaurant and went south. This favor was the least that she could do for Jimmy after he had paid off the house she lived in across town. She knew it was the right thing to do, watching over Jimmy's only child, but enough was enough! Freddy Rosco could wear down the patience of a saint.

"Grandma, we're out of grated cheese!" whined Freddy.

"No, we're not. I'll get some more from the pantry," Rosa said. She sighed as she stood up from the table. Only two more days and she could return to the peace and quiet of her own place. After Friday, Freddy would be someone else's problem.

Chapter Three

The winter gray gave way to warm sunlight and life at the Beach marched on for the Rosco families. Mel, Rita and the kids managed to make about four hundred dollars over the winter from the Shack opening a few hours on Sunday afternoons. It was enough to pay the bills and buy food to tide them over until "the season." There were many dinners created from leftover hotdogs and hamburger patties: pasta with sliced hotdogs and everything imaginable from the ground meat. Meal times were always the same, though — a time to eat and discuss the day's events like most families do. Mel rarely spoke much around the dinner table, allowing instead for Rita to lead the course of discussion.

"Sylvia, I'll help you hem that skirt after dinner if you'd like," said Rita.

"OK, Mom, if you have the time," replied Sylvia. This was Rita's way of ensuring that Sylvia didn't raise her hemline a little too far for school standards as was the trend. The school principal had already called Rita twice to complain about it and she felt embarrassed at having to talk to the man again. The young women were in competition, showing off their thighs to the boys, and in Sylvia's case she had a great set of pipes. No problem, though, because if Mom was too conservative with her needle and thread, Sylvia knew that she and her girlfriends could make it right with a few safety pins and scotch tape in the girls' restroom between classes.

"How are those model cars coming, boys?" Rita asked.

"Mine's almost done," boasted Dickie, "but Donny hasn't started his yet." Donny and Dickie would normally take two of their five dollars earned at the Shack and buy a model car to assemble. They had their own private collection of coupes, dragsters, and pickup trucks. There wasn't much worth watching on television and after the homework was done, this was how they passed the time. Mel and Rita had done their best with their little family and they both wanted their kids would go to college and find a better life than they all had now. The odds were against that, however. Kids from Woodland Beach rarely went past high school and about half the town's residents were dropouts.

School would let out in two weeks and the season would be in full swing on the lake. Campers would descend from all directions to grab some relaxation and time away from their drab routines. Mel opened the Shack for business every day between Memorial Day and Labor Day. Those ten weeks were the time to "make his nut," as he would say. The bank had been pretty good about carrying his loans through the lean winter months, but now it was time for him to catch up. As much as everyone liked Mel, business was business. The bank vice president had personally called him in May, stating that the bank would give him and Rita until October to bring their mortgages up to date. After that, foreclosure seemed the only option. Weather, the economy, and just plain luck would determine the Roscos' financial fate.

Despite his brother being one of the wealthiest men in town, Mel had decided long ago to never ask him for so much as a nickel.

At the same time, things could not have been better for Jimmy and Diane Rosco. The trip to Florida had long since passed, but not without its positive effects. Diane came back up north darkened from the sun's rays and was able to prance around town for a couple weeks until her tan faded. Her skin would darken again up north, eventually, but it wasn't the same. Without cabana boys at her call and the smell of the ocean air, Woodland Beach left her a little flat. While Diane had been indulging herself, Jimmy had found a few items to borrow from the Florida restaurant scene and the new Hawaiian chicken plate was an instant hit at the Shoreline.

Financially speaking, The Shoreline Inn was a real cash cow. Jimmy had recently boosted his bottom line when he finagled a deal with the village to lower his property taxes. By allowing a small corner of his lot to be used as a public right of way to the beach, he had convinced the trustees to lower his tax assessment by twenty percent. Jimmy had the Midas touch when it came to his business.

"That's the least we could do for the guy," concluded one member of the review board. "Look at all the people who come to the Beach to eat at the Shoreline. They spend money at other businesses, too." The review board was right. The Shoreline was an institution and the only decent place to get a sit down meal at the Beach.

As Jimmy had left the township hall, a board member had whispered to him, "Jimmy, see what you can do to get Mel to pay his taxes, will you? He's two years behind." Jimmy didn't say a word but simply lowered his head in disgust. *Mel is on his own*, he thought. *If the guy can't balance his books then he has no right being in the business. Planning, strategy and hard work, that's what separates the winners from the losers.*

Jimmy Rosco felt confident; his bank account was flush and he always had his eyes open for another investment. If the Shack went into default, he'd be the first in line to claim the prize.

Chapter Four

Jimmy Rosco had never cared much for his younger brother Mel. *Why bother?* he thought. They weren't really full brothers and they didn't have a lot in common, other than the fact that they shared the same father.

Frank Rosco had been an old-school type of guy who made money with his hands; construction, machinery, whatever it was, Frank Rosco could usually build or repair it. He took extra shifts at the silverware plant and always had a few side jobs going around town. Frank never let his lack of formal education hold him back: he was a go-getter.

Jimmy's first memories of his father were of him working in the garage after dinner. Frank would put in a full day at the plant, spend a half hour eating with Rosa and his son, and then head out to his shop. Locals knew that Frank had "good hands." The tasks that most folks lacked either the knowledge or time to do were what kept Frank busy. He couldn't count the number of window screens he had replaced, bookshelves he had hung, or car mufflers he had repaired. In the end it didn't matter what the work was, the result was always the same: more cash in his pocket.

Occasionally, Frank let Jimmy help by fetching a tool or sweeping the garage floor. Once in a blue moon he took his son with him to a job site. Jimmy always waited patiently in the car, not wanting to get in the way while his dad worked. Even if only for small scraps of time, Jimmy loved being around his father.

Young Jimmy took on many of Frank's mannerisms. He saw how much emphasis his father put on hard work and tried as a child to mimic his workaholic methods. There was always plenty of work for those who hustled, he surmised. Whether he was rummaging for discarded glass bottles or shoveling a neighbor's driveway, Jimmy Rosco always found a way to make money.

Jimmy was eight years old when Mel came into his life. Happy as an only child, he consumed most of his mother's affection and what little his father saw fit to throw his way. All Rosa wanted out of life was a safe and loving home, but Frank had other ideas. He was convinced that the lone solution to his family's happiness was more money, when in fact the answer was much simpler. A walk in the park, an easy conversation around the kitchen table, this was all it would have taken to satisfy his family, but Frank could never see it that way. Instead, it was easier to just bolt out of bed every morning and work until he was ready to drop. Rosa tried to reason with her husband but Frank only dug in his heels and worked harder. Sometimes he wouldn't come home at night. The spark that he and Rosa had felt as teenage newlyweds faded and life became colorless.

It was not a total surprise to Rosa when Frank, exhausted, finally broke down one night. He admitted that he'd had an affair with a bar maid at one of the watering holes near the silverware plant. In his mind, the indiscretion was nothing more than a short fling, but it had lasted long enough for the young lady to become pregnant. When the girl decided to keep the child, she made it clear that she expected Frank to help support her and the baby. She told Frank that she had no desire to destroy his marriage, but she wasn't going away, either. For a while, they managed to keep their arrangement a secret as Frank struggled to lead a double life and support two families.

After his confession to Rosa, Frank confronted his mistress and told her he could no longer continue. The girl knew there was no way that she could provide for herself and the baby on a bartender's pay. She had no family in the area to help, and the thought of spending life as an unwed mother proved too much for her. In an act of desperation, she abandoned the young boy.

When little three-year-old Melvin showed up at the Roscos' doorstep early one June morning, Rosa's kind and gentle soul took over as she scooped up the crying youngster into her arms. At first she had no idea who he belonged to, but when she turned and saw the pallid look on her husband's face, Rosa knew the answer.

Frank attempted to locate Mel's mother but she had disappeared. No one at the bar knew for sure where she was, either. As Rosa continued to soothe the frightened child, she concluded that turning him over to the authorities would surely sentence him to a life in foster homes. Her faith led her to believe that this might be God's way of healing the wounds that Frank had created, and maybe having a brother would be good for Jimmy.

"You're his father, Frank. His mother has already disregarded him; how can you do the same? What you did was sinful, but turning your back on this little boy now would be even worse," Rosa pleaded. She put love and compassion above her own selfish pride. If Melvin's mother ever returned for him that would be fine, but protecting the young boy was the right thing to do now. It didn't take long for her to decide: she and Frank would keep Mel.

At first, things went well with a new child in the family. Frank cut back on his work obsession and Rosa began to have hope that maybe everything would work out. Jimmy was distant to his new brother in the beginning, but slowly warmed to the idea. A couple years down the road, however, life turned bad again for the Roscos.

The Great Depression slid its grip slowly over the throat of the Northeast. Work became hard to find and Frank was laid off from his manufacturing job. Within a couple of months Frank and Rosa were broke. Hard work was the only lifeline Frank had ever known and without a way to make a living he entered a period of hopelessness and despair. He was too proud to beg or ask for help from relatives who were hurting just as badly. Like so many other downtrodden men, Frank started drinking heavily and the family dynamics crumbled. Angst and despair took hold of his mind and his body, and his spirit gave way to defeat. Rather than stick it out, Frank chose to run away from his wife, his children, and his home.

When he learned of growing job opportunities in the Georgia paper mills, he didn't think to ask Rosa about moving. He wanted to escape and start anew. Once he found success down south he could eventually get her and the boys to join him, but for now, he had to do this for himself. He would send money back to his wife and boys. Rosa had friends and neighbors to help her, he reasoned, and unlike Mel's mother, he was sure that his wife would put the boys first and raise them properly while he was gone.

At 3 a.m. on a crisp March morning, Frank Rosco crept out of his house with only the clothes on his back and an empty heart that raced inside his chest. A pickup truck carrying two of his single buddies from the plant quietly pulled up and he got inside.

The truck headed south, leaving behind a wife, two young sons, and a trail of lost dreams.

Frank Rosco would never return.

When Rosa woke up that morning, she assumed that Frank had left the house early in search of some work to do around town. While making a pot of coffee she found his note.

"Dear Rosa, I can't take this life anymore and need to make a change. I am headed down south to find work."

In the envelope she found two twenty dollar bills that Frank had reaped from selling off most of his tools. Three weeks passed before she heard from him. When a letter in his handwriting arrived, she tore it open.

"Dear Rosa, I found work outside of Augusta, Georgia. Please give my boys a hug. I will write again soon. Love, Frank."

Rosa wished there was more to read. She wondered, *Where are you staying? When will you be back?* There were two more twenty dollar bills inside the envelope but the money was a small consolation for the man she still loved. She took a deep breath and searched for what she could tell the boys. Until now she had suspected that Frank might be gone forever, but this gave her hope.

The next day, after getting Jimmy off to school, a police car turned into her driveway. She finished pouring Mel's cereal and walked to the window. Rosa recognized the state trooper who stepped out from the vehicle. He looked somber as he turned and said something across the roof of the car to a woman getting out of the passenger side. When Rosa saw the parish priest emerge from the back seat she felt faint. She knew instantly that something had happened to her husband.

Frank Rosco was killed in an accident at the paper mill. He had been doing double shifts since hiring on at the plant. Two nights prior, while driving his forklift outside the mill, he stopped to help another worker who was preparing to unload a truckload of pine logs. A restraining bracket holding the logs on the truck gave way, the load shifted, and a dozen four hundred pound timbers tumbled down. The other man was lucky and survived with only a broken ankle, but Frank Rosco was crushed to death.

After the death of her husband, Rosa continued to treat Mel as her own. The bitter fact that the boy was illegitimate slowly faded in the mind of the community and people accepted Rosa for what she truly was, an unfortunate young widow raising two sons. She worked a variety of jobs and the family scraped by.

Sadly, although they were half brothers and lived under the same roof, Jimmy developed a seething resentment for Mel. Not only did he blame him for their father's departure, but he also begrudged his brother's popularity. For as serious and self-centered a person as Jimmy Rosco was, Mel was a happy-go-lucky spirit who required very little to keep him happy. He made friends easily while Jimmy was a loner. As the boys grew older they spent little time together. The five-year age difference only widened the gap between them.

It was really only a coincidence that both ran businesses at the Beach as adults.

Jimmy's Shoreline Inn and Rosco's Fry Shack were as opposite as one could imagine and a direct reflection of the type of man that owned them. From the beginning, their contradictory personalities would take them down dissimilar paths. Only fate could cause a convergence.

Chapter Five

"Morning, Donny. Coffee, regular please," said Steve. Donny Rosco had just finished brewing the first pot of the day and as usual Steve Mills was his first customer. "Coffee, regular" was the term everyone at the Beach used to order a cup of coffee with cream and sugar. That was the only thing Steve ordered at the Shack — no food, ever. He was always outside the concession stand at the same time every morning, 9:30 sharp. None of the other businesses at the park opened until 10 or 11 and the Shack would go through four or five pots of coffee every day before noon. Mel said that he never made much profit off the beverage, but nonetheless opened his place earlier than the others at the park, primarily for those in search of their morning cup.

Steve was the manager at the Lakeshore Hotel across the street from the Shack. Donny couldn't remember ever meeting anyone who had actually paid for a room at the Lakeshore. Supposedly, many years ago the place had been a nice spot to stay and afforded guests great views of the lake and cool, gentle night-time breezes during the humid summer months. Built at the turn of the century, it had offered guests a reasonably priced night's stay and a full service restaurant. Over the years, however, it had steadily declined from resort-like status to its present state: a loud rock and roll joint. Places like the Lakeshore were filled with rowdy, intoxicated crowds reminiscent of an old Western saloon, and there was not a more experienced saloon guy than Steve Mills. He had started out thirty-five years ago in the business, first as a bouncer, then a bartender, and now he ran day-to-day operations at the Lakeshore during its three month season. Steve would appear at the Beach every spring and quietly disappear in the fall. Nobody knew exactly where he went, but most folks suspected that he headed south. When someone would try to pin him down as to his plans for the off-season, he predictably mumbled something like, "Oh, I'll be here and there. Not really sure right now."

When Steve walked across the street to order his coffee he was sucking on his fifth cigarette of the day. The morning jolt of caffeine was a ritual for both him and Donny, more or less signifying the start of another day. Steve always looked the same: shiny black hair combed straight back and wearing the same outfit, a starched white shirt and black trousers. Donny imagined that in the closet of Steve's small room at the Lakeshore was a collection of white shirts lined up neatly alongside an equal number of black pants. *Nothing fancy for this guy,* thought Donny. Dress simply, get the job done, and close down the joint after Labor Day.

Steve was one of the many characters that Mel Rosco affectionately thought of as "beach rats." These people were the ones who showed up every spring to run the amusement rides, games, eateries, and joints. Most were what outsiders referred to as "carnies." These men and women roamed the East Coast working the carnivals, state fairs, and festivals. In the wintertime, most migrated south in search of sun and warmer weather along the carnival circuit; Charlotte, Charleston, Savannah, wherever there was work to be done and a few bucks to be made. In the summertime Woodland Beach offered them plenty of work and a relief from the nomadic life of being on the run.

Steve ran the Lakeshore with a couple of other beach rats who also resided in the old clapboard building for the summer — Willis Shank, who was a talented maintenance guy, and another fellow named Laparco. Laparco's first name was actually Anthony, but hardly anyone around the midway ever called him by his given name. He was simply "Laparco" and served as the janitor at the Lakeshore. He filled in when Willis needed a hand with building maintenance and ran errands for Steve. Neither Willis nor Laparco had much formal education past elementary school, but they were good employees whom Steve counted on. Most importantly, they were loyal and honest. Steve had learned over decades of being a saloon guy that nothing destroyed the bottom line faster than untrustworthy help.

"Are you ready for the Fourth, Donny?" asked Steve. He grasped the paper cup full of coffee and blew gently across the top to cool it down.

"As ready as I'll ever be," Donny answered. "My dad's anticipating big things this weekend. He ordered five more fifty pound bags of potatoes."

"Well, you'll probably need them," Steve replied. "It's a golden weekend."

July Fourth fell on a Monday this year and that was the best of all situations for businesses at the Beach. There would be four big days, Friday through Monday, concluding with fireworks over the lake on July Fourth. The local merchants viewed this holiday weekend as a "make it or break it" time for the year. Although the summer season spanned a full ten weeks, the Fourth of July always defined how successful the summer was. A good four day weekend around the Fourth was truly "golden." The Beach's population swelled to several thousand residents during the summer as campers descended on the lakefront town. Many more would drive in for day trips.

As the "open-up" guy, Donny worked Monday through Friday from nine to five. A group of older fellows came in to handle the busier night shift at the Shack. Dickie would help him three days during the week, but being three years younger than Donny at twelve, Mel was conscientious of letting the younger brother enjoy more of his summer vacation. At times Donny wished that he didn't work so much and was able to spend summer vacation like most of his schoolmates. It was hard for him to watch his friends take advantage of the fun a lake had to offer. Over the summer months he would do a little swimming and fishing but the family business took a priority.

There were, however, some benefits to his job. The Shack was situated at the most visited area of the amusement park, what Mel called the "action corner" where three different streets intersected. When you visited the Beach, most likely you either walked or drove by the Shack. For Donny, this meant lots of pretty girls would pass by him on their way to the water or the amusement rides while he worked. Many stopped to buy something to eat or drink. He never had a problem meeting cute young ladies, most of whom were on vacation and in search of fun. Being on the other side of the counter provided him with a sort of free license to make small talk with them in a way he never would have dared to do otherwise. Donny enjoyed his daily routine as the open-up guy and Mel paid him the going rate — minimum wage of one dollar and five cents per hour plus tips.

It was Wednesday and things were shaping up to be a great week. The weather forecast called for warm and humid temperatures, which meant people would flock to the lake in droves.

Mel ordered the Shack's operations to be at full strength for the entire weekend. Dickie and Donny would be joined by the older guys, Carl, Ron, and Ollie, during the daytime shift. Mel planned to fill in as needed throughout the weekend.

"See you later," Donny called out as Steve walked away, coffee in hand and smoke number six freshly lit. "Say hello to Willis and Laparco for me."

"Will do, Donny," Steve acknowledged. He didn't turn around but waved goodbye with his free hand as he ambled back to work.

Chapter Six

The line of people stretched twenty yards down the sidewalk outside of Jimmy's Shoreline Inn. The aroma of fried fish stretched even farther. Jimmy's place was known for its deep fried haddock and today was Friday, fish day. Folks traveled from fifty miles away for the pleasure of dining at the Shoreline. The drive to the lake was always pleasant for those escaping from the routine in their cities and towns. And after all, Jimmy's was the only decent sit-down place to eat at the Beach. Amidst the hot dog stands, concessions, and joints, Jimmy's offered patrons a place with a little class. That's why customers rarely griped about the long waits. There were two lines of customers formed outside the building, directed by two signs: "Parties of four or less, line forms here" and "Parties of five or more, line forms here." This was Jimmy Rosco's idea and served as another example of how efficiently he ran his business.

He had also fine-tuned his menu to predict how many of certain entrees would sell on any given day of the week, thus streamlining his inventory of supplies. Sunday was a big breakfast day after church. Monday was the slowest day of the week and he reduced his staff by twenty percent. Tuesday night was when the Shoreline sold the most ice cream. On Wednesday, for some odd reason, sales of the hamburger and fries plate were greater than other days. On Thursday he ran his barbeque special and of course Friday was the fried fish platter. Saturday was always a roll of the dice depending on the crowd. The new Hawaiian chicken dish he had copied from down south was a featured special on Saturday nights and it was showing great promise.

Jimmy Rosco managed his establishment like a pro football coach roaming the sidelines. To him, strategy, planning, and preparation separated the winners and losers in this business. There was nothing he left to chance, even the details of how his waitresses dressed. The entire wait staff was comprised of middle-aged females who wore white nurse-like uniforms complete with white stockings. Likewise, the kitchen was staffed entirely by females. He did employ a few males as busboys and counter help, but his most loyal and reliable workers were the women. Rosa Rosco had recruited most of them years ago, and Jimmy relied on referrals from his current employees when there was an opening to fill.

Working at Jimmy's Shoreline Inn was a sign of status at the Beach. Most of his waitresses were locals and many would walk through town on their way to work. It was a familiar sight for residents to notice the parade of twenty or so mature women making their way to and from work throughout the day. They wore their crisp uniforms proudly, not unlike a veteran soldier who has earned his stripes. They didn't need insignia or emblems, though; the starched white outfit was their badge of honor. For many, working at the Shoreline would prove to be the most rewarding, best paying job of their lives. Jimmy paid well and most customers tipped generously because they considered it a privilege to dine there.

Mel never quite understood the big attraction at Jimmy's: the food was average at best, in his opinion. He wondered how his brother had become so successful as he scratched out a living three months a year at the Shack. His time during the off-season was spent repairing his equipment or looking for odd jobs around town. Other than the money they earned when lugging the green water can on winter Sundays, the family relied on Rita's part time job at the post office to supplement their income during the off-season. Mel was fortunate to have a hard working family and secretly felt sorry for Jimmy, who was stuck with sun goddess Diane and Fat Freddy. Those two did nothing but take, although with Jimmy's success, he had plenty to give.

Despite all that his brother possessed, Mel knew that deep down Jimmy was a sad, lonely guy. *If that was what big money brought, then I want no part of it*, thought Mel. He was happy with his life as it was. Donny was now old enough to open up the Shack on weekdays, allowing Mel free time to run errands, order supplies and tend to the small arcade he was developing next to the Shack — "coin operated amusements," as he referred to them. Mel planned for his daughter Sylvia to work as a cashier when he opened the arcade for the first time this weekend. Over the years Sylvia had begged him to let her work at the Shack, but Mel couldn't fathom the thought of his daughter sweating it out in the hot, greasy place.

Overall, Mel felt pretty lucky. The new season brought a renewed hope that he and Rita would pull out of the downward financial spiral they were in.

Chapter Seven

"Dad, I need a couple bucks to fill up the mini bike," said Freddy. As promised, upon returning from Florida, Jimmy had bought his son a new motorized toy. A cross between a scooter and a motorcycle, Freddy's new plaything was his pride and joy, and as usual, he was the first kid in town to own one.

"Freddy, it only takes seventy-five cents to fill the thing," replied Jimmy.

"I know, but I need some extra money to buy a snack later," answered Freddy. Jimmy relented and handed over two dollars. It would be easier to just give in to the whiny kid. If not, the rest of the day would be miserable for him and Diane.

"Be careful on that thing, OK?" asked Jimmy.

"Sure, Dad. I'll look both ways at intersections and not speed," he said with mocked sincerity as he revved the bike's noisy motor. Freddy sped away and mapped out his itinerary for the afternoon. He would gas up and then cruise down Park Avenue along the beachfront leading to the amusement park where the Shack was located. Young girls always congregated at the Action Corner by his uncle's place and it was a great spot to show off on his new ride. Freddy took in the sights along the quarter mile drive. People of all ages were enjoying the sunny, warm Friday afternoon. The sky was blue and a light breeze created small whitecaps on the waves: the scene reminded many visitors of the ocean. Indian Lake was famous for its wide, sandy beachfront and hard-packed, sandy bottom, something uncommon at other lakes in the area where rock-filled beaches and mucky bottoms were the norm. Swimmers and waders loved coming here.

Freddy was still too immature to grasp the fact that these people who came to the Beach to spend money were actually the same people who had helped pay for his shiny new mini bike. Jimmy had tried to get Freddy interested in working at the restaurant after he turned twelve, but the kid was so spoiled rotten it was no use. Jimmy and Diane hoped that once Freddy was in high school he might become more motivated and find some direction. In the meantime, however, it was easier for them to give in to his wishes. They were both too occupied to do otherwise.

Freddy was full of himself as he rounded the corner in front of the Shack. Sure enough, as expected, a group of teenage girls was sitting idly on the red stools along the counter. He came to a stop directly in front of the hot dog grill where his cousin was standing, gunned the bike's motor a few times and smiled at the girls.

Carl Wilcox was laughing so hard, he had to pull the car to the side of the road. Ron wasn't much help, egging on his lifelong buddy and not letting up as they rehashed the details of another ballsy high school stunt. This one involved lying to their mothers about sleeping over at each other's houses when in fact they had stayed out all night and drove to Canada for a cup of coffee.

It was all done on a dare, with nothing more at stake than proving they could get away with it. Unfortunately, the two girls they convinced to go with them got caught and were grounded for a month. Carl and Ron went unscathed.

Carl settled back into driving and refocused on testing out the new clutch he had installed earlier that morning. After finding a quiet two-laner rarely used by anyone, he commenced a series of clutch popping, speed shifting drills he had devised himself. A self taught mechanic, this was Carl's fourth car. He proudly wore the moniker of "grease monkey" and knew his way around his dad's garage by age twelve.

After scanning in both direction to verify no one was watching, Carl put the clutch to the floor, placed the car's steering column-mounted shifter in first gear, revved the engine just shy of the tachometer's redline and let out the clutch gently. The big V8 motor unleashed its horsepower, the energy rushed through the car's transmission, drive shaft, and axle, finally reaching the small spot where the tire rubber met the road. The rear wheels screamed out, initially able to hold only a fraction of the force; the car fished tailed slightly to the left as blue-white smoke poured out from the vehicle's back end.

After a half dozen cycles of engine revving, powering through all three gears, and then down shifting to a stop, Carl looked at his watch and decided it was time to head to work at Mel's.

"Yeah, that'll do," he said confidently, nodding his head with approval. Another quick glance in his mirror confirmed that no one was following him and the six separate clouds of burnt rubber had dissipated. Reaching the main road, they spotted a state police cruiser parked off the side. Both boys calmly said the word "cop," more as an involuntary response than a caution. Carl shifted smoothly and accelerated past the officer who had just

issued a speeding ticket to a family returning home from an afternoon at the lake — a wonderful day in the sun spoiled when the
happy, relaxed father exceeded the posted limit by ten miles per
hour and fell prey to a speed trap.

The officer looked up when he heard the throaty rumble of
the car's dual exhaust pipes. He saw exactly what he expected: the
familiar sight of a blue and white '58 Buick driven by "that punk
Wilcox." Knowing full well he was being watched, Carl checked
his speedometer: thirty-five miles per hour, precisely five under
the limit. Carl could almost feel the officer's scowl as he and Ron
glided past. He recognized the cop as the one who had popped
him six months ago on a real chicken shit offense: failure to come
to a complete stop at an intersection. The infraction had
occurred on a quiet country road at night, prompting Carl to
wonder, *Don't you have something better to do, asshole?*

"Fuck you," Carl uttered under his breath at the officer
when safely clear of the patrol car. The two boys were quiet as
Carl's anger subsided and the car slowly picked up speed.

"Hey Carl, stop and give this guy a ride, will ya? He looks
familiar," Ron said. A tall, thin boy was walking along the road
up ahead.

"Who is it?" Carl asked.

"I don't know his name, but I've seen him around the Beach
all summer. He's thumbing on this road almost every day."

Carl guided the car onto the shoulder and waved for the
young man to hop in the car's rear seat. He noticed that the guy
had worked up a good sweat walking in the hot afternoon sun.

"Hey, thanks guys, it's hot out here today," said the hitchhiker.

"No problem. Don't sit on those clothes, just slide them over
to the other side," Ron said, referring to the fresh pairs of cut off
jeans and sport shirts he and Carl had brought along for later.
They were both wearing white tee shirts emblazoned with "The

Shack" on the front and back. For the first season ever, Mel had ordered the shirts for his employees, breaking the long-standing tradition of his crew wearing plain white tees. Despite the heat, Mel also asked his help to wear long pants, something Ron and Carl protested vehemently at first, threatening to quit. Mel insisted, however, fearing someone might splash hot oil from the fryers on their legs. In effect, the long pants requirement was about the only restriction Mel put on his help. Otherwise, he ran things pretty loosely and over the years had enjoyed having loyal, hard-working crews.

The three rode silently for a minute until Ron finally spoke up. "Where you going?"

"The Beach, my girlfriend lives there. My name is John," the teen answered, extending his hand to shake over the front seat. He welcomed the breeze coming in from the car window: it felt good against his damp dress shirt. John had walked three of the eight miles from his house, and this was the third car he'd hitched on as he criss-crossed his way to the Beach. He hoped his sweaty shirt dried out before he got to his girl's house.

"Oh yeah, what's her name?" Carl asked. Woodland Beach was a small town and he and Ron knew just about every good-looking teenage girl within a ten mile radius. Carl thought to himself, *Who is this yokel moving in on our territory?*

"Her name is Sylvia, Sylvia Rosco," the rider answered.

Carl and Ron turned toward the hitchhiker with stunned looks on their faces. They both had a crush on their boss's pretty daughter, secretly wishing she was a little older and not related to Mel Rosco. Ron and Carl were a couple of hounds when it came to the ladies, but they kept a polite distance from Sylvia, considering her off limits. During their five years of working at the Shack, they had watched Sylvia Rosco mature from a gawky, common looking kid into a curvy young beauty.

Turning his eyes back to the road, Carl said, "You're a lucky guy. Sylvia is a great girl." Normally, when talking about one of the local honeys, he and Ron would have launched into a detailed analysis of the girl's physical attributes, debated their chances of "getting lucky," and discussed the prevailing word on the street about her. They had too much respect for Mel and his family to take the conversation in that direction, however.

After their initial introductions, the threesome spent the rest of the drive discussing cars, and the upcoming weekend at the Beach. Carl went into detail about his new clutch installation and John told Ron and Carl he was in the process of working on a car himself; this ordeal of bumming rides to see his girlfriend was getting old. His folks had only one vehicle and he was on the bottom of the priority list to use it.

Coming over the canal bridge, the three noted how busy the amusement park was. The time was 4:45 and the parking lot was already half full.

"Man, this place is hopping already," Carl said as he slowed down, conscious of another speed trap at the bottom of the bridge. The quickest route to the Shack was to come over the canal, make a sharp right turn and wind back underneath the bridge. Then it was a short drive traveling along the canal, through the Action Corner, and finally into the parking lot. Today, however, he and Ron were fifteen minutes early, and wanting to do Sylvia's boyfriend a favor, Carl decided to drive out of his way and take John directly to the Roscos'.

"Hey, thanks again," John said as he got out the car.

"Don't mention it," returned Carl. Ron looked up and saw Sylvia waiting in the doorway, her hair still in curlers. She smiled at the three of them and waved as Carl lightly revved the Buick's engine. He waved back and popped the clutch gingerly, producing a short, one-second tire squeal that punctuated his goodbye.

The two drove down Park Avenue by the waterfront, catching the sights along the way: people of all shapes and sizes enjoying the sunny summer day, children eating cotton candy and young girls in bikinis. Carl took his time maneuvering down the crowded street, avoiding the Action Corner altogether on this back route. Walking the short distance from the parking lot, they were greeted by the whiff of fries and hamburgers cooking at the Shack.

"Ah, shit! Look who's here," Ron moaned at the sight of Fat Freddy ripping across the Action Corner on his mini bike.

"Man, that's it. Not today," said Carl. He shook his head and motioned Ron to follow him through the woods leading to the Shack's back door.

Chapter Eight

"Hey, Donny, when are you going to get a bike like this?" taunted Freddy. Donny looked up from refilling the bun warmer and turned his attention to his cousin. The girls continued talking amongst themselves, occasionally looking toward Freddy who returned their glances with a dumb, confident grin.

Donny had to shout over the rap-tap-tap noise of the bike. "Never. I'll wait another year and get my driver's license instead."

Freddy didn't respond but instead laughed defiantly and tore off toward the lake, starring back at Donny as he accelerated. He built up speed and decided to put on a little show for the benefit of the girls who had stopped chatting now and turned their attention in his direction. Freddy had mastered doing little wheelies with his machine, so back and forth he went doing the same stunt over and over until it grew stale. The young girls went back to their conversation and no one paid any further attention to his display.

Finally Donny shouted again over the commotion, "Freddy, enough already, go somewhere else and make noise!" Freddy pointed to his left ear and shook his head disdainfully, pretending he couldn't hear. The girls had lost all interest by now and ignored him completely. This only made him more determined as he took off again and resorted to simply blasting back and forth at full throttle in front of the Shack. A lady who approached the counter to buy drinks for her children abruptly stopped and dragged the kids away, fearing that Freddy might hit them. After a few minutes of this, Donny realized that Freddy was scaring off customers.

Donny checked his watch. The older guys were due in any moment to relieve him. Maybe they could help. Freddy had thrown small tantrums in the past but nothing ever like this. About the time he decided to reach for the phone to call his father, he heard the sound of rumbling on the roof. Phone in hand, he looked up in time to see Freddy getting drenched by a deluge of water pouring down from above.

"Get the hell out of the road, fat ass!" two voices hollered from above. Having witnessed the Fat Freddy show on the way to work, Ron and Carl had decided to take the situation into their own hands by lugging two water buckets up to the roof. They hid behind the "Rosco's Fry Shack" sign and when Freddy slowed down to reverse course, they sprang out and doused him good. Although he was barely moving at the time, the cold water startled him to the point of losing his balance and he fell off his bike. Freddy's ample butt hit the pavement with no more force than a person gently plopping down into a chair, but nonetheless this prompted him to launch into one of his famous tirades. He bleated like a wounded animal as he sat there drenched, next to his fallen chariot. The girls were less than ten feet away and began laughing hysterically.

His face now beet-red, Freddy's eyes bolted from the girls, to Carl and Ron above and then to Donny, who was grinning from ear to ear and struggling to contain his laughter. Seeing Donny only made things worse, as Freddy now kicked his howl into a full blown shriek. He stumbled to his feet, feigned a dramatic limp and shuffled off the road onto the sidewalk. The embarrassed look on his face changed instantly to a bug-eyed glare, as he turned to his cousin and screamed, "I'll get you for this Donny, you and your greasy family! I'll get you!"

The girls stopped laughing and stared at him in disbelief.

"Go on home, Freddy, you big baby," Carl said calmly. With that, Freddy pivoted and started running in the direction of home. He ran for about thirty yards until his bulk overcame his energy and he settled into a slow shuffle. His whole body jiggled as he waddled away, oblivious to his treasured mini bike abandoned on the side of the road. Donny jumped over the counter and wheeled it into the alley next to the Shack.

"Why did you guys do that?" Donny asked.

"He'll be all right, Donny," said Ron, now down from the rooftop. "Christ, we had to do something. He's been pulling that routine all week; you must have missed it. He almost hit a little girl riding her bicycle yesterday."

"A splash of cold water never hurt anyone," added Carl. The two older guys laughed and settled into work: Carl brewed a fresh pot of coffee and Ron checked the temperature controls on the deep fryers.

As Donny walked home, the sight of blue sky and the lake's foaming waves was lost while he sorted out what had just happened, and how he could have prevented it. He had a bad feeling that Freddy was going to cause some trouble. Carl and Ron thought it was a big joke, but Donny knew better. Freddy Rosco was a mean kid and someone was going to pay.

"Why didn't you call me?" asked Mel.

"I tried to, Dad, but it was too late. By the time I picked up the phone Carl and Ron already got him."

Mel tolerated Freddy's bad behavior the way everybody else did and he knew all too well about the kid's temper. Although Mel and Jimmy rarely spoke anymore, their wives did. Rita and Diane maintained a cool but civil relationship, due mainly to Rita's job at the village post office. It was near impossible for her not to make small talk when standing at the counter as people came in to buy stamps or mail a package. When Diane came into the post office the conversation would invariably turn to the children and she frequently let on what a hassle Freddy could be. Rita listened patiently, all the while thinking to herself, *Diane, if you spent half the time with the kid as you do shopping or working on your tan, the boy might behave a little better.* After Diane unloaded her gripes and left, Rita thanked God that Sylvia, Donny and Dickie were her children and Freddy Rosco belonged to someone else.

Mel listened quietly to his son's explanation of what had happened. "I guess there wasn't much you could do to stop it. I'll talk to Ron and Carl later," he said. Donny started climbing the stairs to his room. Halfway up, he paused and overheard his parents talking.

"Rita, do you think you could call Diane to see if Freddy is OK?"

"If I have to," Rita answered grudgingly. She sensed that any words with Diane about what had occurred would be a lose-lose proposition, but she was willing to try. It was the most important weekend of the year for their business and the last thing she and Mel needed now was a family squabble.

"I'll call her and try to calm the waters, but it never seems to help with those people. They look down their noses at us and Diane will turn this into something more than what it is."

"Honey, we can't just ignore it," pleaded Mel. Rita saw the fatigue and worry in his face. The guy had been working sixteen-hour days for two weeks and didn't have the strength to argue, but he knew the right thing to do. Rita was the only person who might be able to smooth things over before Freddy did something stupid.

When he got mad about something, not only was Freddy Rosco capable of doing something stupid, he could be flat out cruel. Three years ago, he had gotten pissed off at one of the neighbor's kids for teasing him and preceded to steal the family's cat. After luring it with food he threw it into a burlap sack, hid it in the woods for the night and then carried it to a remote bridge early one morning. Sure that no one was watching, he opened up the sack and dumped the cat out over the side. The disoriented animal plunged thirty feet down to the water and hit with a violent splat. Stunned and winded, it scrambled desperately to stay afloat and survive. Miraculously, a fisherman who had tied up his boat under the bridge heard the splash and paddled over to see what the commotion was. He scooped up the poor animal with his fishing net and the cat lived. Freddy, watching the scene from above, panicked and fled, but not before the fisherman recognized him and confronted Jimmy with the event later that day.

As was normally the case, Jimmy and Diane were incredulous that their son could do such a thing. Freddy concocted a story that the cat must have ran away, and while taking a morning bike ride he saw the animal on the bridge and tried to coax it into his grasp. According to Freddy, the cat then scurried away afraid, and accidentally fell off the bridge.

Freddy didn't have a good explanation for why he was riding his bike two miles from home at 6:15 in the morning. Nonetheless, after returning the cat to its owners, Jimmy offered both the family and the fisherman a complimentary meal at the Shoreline as a gesture of friendship. Both parties accepted, but remained skeptical. Now that Freddy was older and more physically imposing, people who knew him generally steered clear. Jimmy and Diane's status in the community served as a screen for their son's bad behavior.

Rita dialed Diane's home number but there was no answer. She made a note to try again in the morning.

As Freddy walked back from the Shack, he hoped that someone would be home when he opened the door. It was 5:30 p.m. but the house was empty. His father would be at the restaurant, of course; where his mother was, he had no idea. Grandma Rosa usually came over on Friday nights to cook dinner for him but even she was not around tonight, having left on a road trip earlier in the day. Freddy shuffled through the kitchen on the way to his bedroom, instinctively grabbing a handful of cookies from a jar as he passed by. Other than the wet squishing sound of his sneakers, the place was silent.

He thought about retrieving his mini bike, but decided against it: his dad would probably dispatch someone to get it when he found out what happened. Engulfed in self-pity, Freddy plopped onto his bed, reached over and turned on the television set.

Chapter Nine

Rosa honked the car horn and smiled. She couldn't remember how many times she'd actually made this trip but guessed it was over a hundred. The habit of honking the horn when she crossed into Pennsylvania had started when the boys were still young. Rosa kept the tradition alive and still shouted out "Welcome to Pennsylvania, the Keeeeeystone State!" the same way Jimmy and Mel had done when they were with her. By age fifteen, however, her oldest child had concluded the entire act was stupid, leaving Rosa and Mel to carry on the ritual, which they did gleefully.

Rosa had never been away from home on the Fourth and wasn't quite sure how this weekend would pan out for her. For so many summers she had been in the thick of it all at Jimmy's supervising his kitchen staff, sometimes logging fifteen hour days like her son. Though she didn't consider herself old, when Jimmy had approached her about retiring from the Shoreline last year, Rosa embraced the idea of slowing down and enjoying herself while she was still healthy enough to do so. Leisurely road trips were one of the few activities she liked doing alone and the bucolic scenery carved out from the rugged New York/Pennsylvania landscape always made her feel happy to be alive.

Just south of the New Milford exit, the roar of a semi blazing past jarred Rosa from her daydreaming. Until now, the traffic had been relatively light and she had rolled down the windows to stay cool, but as the day progressed, the highway cacophony grew. Cars and trucks raced by her, their drivers anxious to claim a slice of the holiday weekend too. Rosa sought relief from the commotion and took the next off ramp. She didn't notice the exit number or what town it led to, but it didn't matter. She knew the way.

"What happened, did you get lost?" Sophie shouted from the porch. Rosa spotted her older sister smiling as she parked the car.

"No, just took the long way, off the interstate through Hop Bottom. The holiday traffic was too noisy and I felt like seeing the countryside today. It's so nice out."

The drive from the Beach to Tunkhannock normally took three hours, door to door. Back when the boys were with her, the route was a patchwork of tedious two-laners, but now with I-81 built, the drive was a snap.

"Well, glad you're here. You can help me pick some tomatoes for dinner. My early season variety is ripe." Sophie took Rosa's suitcase and set it inside the house. Rosa loved the easygoing feeling of her sister's farm. Her life at Woodland Beach was comfortable and the small brick ranch Jimmy had built for her was nice, but this was where she felt the best about herself. Her "neat as a pin" little place was the complete opposite of Sophie's, where dishes sometimes sat in the sink for a couple days and chickens roamed the yard freely. Still, there was nowhere on earth that Rosa Marie Rosco felt safer than here with her big sister.

"Sauce tonight?" Rosa asked. She held a wooden basket while Sophie bent over and picked the plum tomatoes. Sophie had constructed a small hothouse on the side of the barn and prided herself at getting a jump on everyone else's garden.

"Yeah, Big Al has a taste for Italian tonight. Gotta keep the old Kraut happy."

Rosa laughed at her sister's blunt jab at her husband. Sophie's earthiness never failed to warm her heart. It had helped keep her going during her darkest days after Frank died and she struggled to raise the boys. The trips south that she made two or three times every year always produced memorable stories and laughter.

"You worried about him leaving you for some hot little honey, Soph?" teased Rosa.

"Nah, that tiger lost his teeth and claws a long time ago," Sophie answered. "He's harmless." Rosa burst out laughing. She knew her sister was only joking about her husband: she worshipped the man. Albert Rolfsheiner had emigrated from Germany in the early 1900s and met Sophie while working for the railroad in central New York. An intensely disciplined man, he told his future bride that once he saved enough money, he planned to buy land west of Scranton near his brother and live as a diary farmer. He kept his word and Sophie followed him to Pennsylvania over forty years ago. Al never smiled or laughed much but had a heart of gold. Growing up, young Mel had loved doing farm chores and sitting on his uncle's lap driving the tractor.

The two women walked inside and began preparing dinner together. Sophie explained that Al had driven into town to buy parts for a combine and that her youngest child, Theresa, would be joining the three of them for dinner in a couple hours.

"Oh, wonderful!" Rosa said. "I was so hoping to see her."

"She has a break from grad school at State and told me not to let you leave without seeing her." Of Sophie's three children, Theresa was the only one still in the area and she held a special place in Rosa's heart. Besides being her goddaughter, Theresa had come into the world at a time when the entire family needed some hope. The country was entering World War Two, Rosa was overwhelmed raising two teenagers, and Al was struggling to keep the farm afloat on the heels of the Depression. Sophie referred to her only daughter as "our little surprise" when she conceived her at age forty.

"How are the boys and their families?" asked Sophie.

"Well, things are about the same for everyone. I don't see Mel, Rita, and the kids that much. Mel stops by now and then for coffee but he's up to his ass in alligators trying to stay in business. I still watch Freddy when Jimmy and Diane ask me to."

"That kid lose any weight yet?" Sophie said. With the tomatoes cooking down, she turned her attention to rolling out a piecrust. Her apron and the kitchen floor were covered in flour but she didn't seem to care.

"No, not really. He just seems to get bigger and bigger," answered Rosa.

"I wish Jimmy and Diane would straighten that kid out. I always said, give him to me and Al for a couple weeks on the farm and that's all it'll take." Sophie shook the rolling pin at Rosa to emphasize her point.

"Jimmy's raising that kid to be just like him, a mean, selfish little . . ."

"Hey, sis, could we change the subject?" Rosa interrupted. "I came down here to see you and Al. Let's not ruin the day."

"OK, hon, you're right. Apple or blueberry? I canned 'em both last fall."

"I think I'd like blueberry pie with my spaghetti tonight, thank you," Rosa said, smiling. Her sister nodded approval. The ladies spent the next hour cooking, joking and retelling the same stories that made them laugh every time. For a few moments they felt young again. Rosa did talk briefly about how spoiled Freddy was. Sophie took it all in, but bit her tongue when she regained the urge to launch into her nephew and his son. She also knew there wasn't a thing she could do to ease the pain her sister felt from the rift between Mel and Jimmy. Any chance of her liking Rosa's oldest son had long since passed. In her mind Jimmy was still the distant, cruel kid she had caught pummeling her hens with stones when he was twelve. Al had invited the boys to ride with him as he delivered morning milk cans to the dairy on Tioga Street in town. Mel clamored into the truck, eager to join his uncle and cousins. Jimmy said that he wasn't interested and drifted off into the barn by himself. When Sophie found him in the chicken coop taking out his frustrations on her hens, she wanted to clobber him but restrained herself. Grabbing him by the hair she got nose to nose and said if she ever caught him pulling a stunt like that again, he'd be sorry he was ever born. From that point on, Jimmy steered clear of his no-nonsense aunt and she watched him like a hawk. Like everyone else, she and Al cherished little Mel and simply tolerated Jimmy. That only widened the divide between the two boys.

"I'm stuffed," declared Al. The big farmer stood up, tugged at his belt as if to loosen it a bit, and walked out on to the porch. On his way, he gently slapped Sophie's butt and said, "Very good, madam, thank you." His wife looked up and smiled back, shaking her head in amusement.

Theresa and Rosa joined Al on the porch while Sophie put together a tray with coffee and pie. The humid air was cooling nicely and the mosquitoes kept their distance. Rosa sat back on the glider and breathed a sigh of relief. It had been a long day.

After dessert, Al settled in to reading the paper and smoking a cigar as the women talked. His routine was predictable: "up at daybreak and asleep at dark." Twenty minutes later, his inner clock signaled the sun sinking behind the ridgeline and he politely excused himself. Fed, current with the day's news, and his nightly smoke finished, Al went to bed.

"Aunt Rosa, tell me about Mel and Jimmy and what's new at the Beach," Theresa said. Rosa repeated much of what she had already told her sister, catching herself when she touched on the animosity between the two families.

"I never understood what the problem was between Jimmy and Mel. Guess I was always too young to understand it and nobody talks about it here." Theresa glanced at her mother. Sophie sat quietly and returned her daughter's look with a raised eyebrow. After a pause, Theresa continued. "What is it between those two, anyway?"

"Tessy, your aunt doesn't need to go into that. I think you should . . ."

"No, that's all right, Soph. We can talk about it. They're her cousins and she has a right to know."

"It's up to you, Ro," Sophie replied.

"You know that Mel and Jimmy are stepbrothers. Your uncle Frank had a girl friend who was Mel's mother. She abandoned him when he was only three years old."

"Yes, I know all of that, but what I could never understand was why you kept him after your husband died. Wouldn't it have been easier on you to just give him up for adoption?"

"Absolutely. I could barely keep food on the table the first couple of years. Without your mom and dad I don't know what would have happened. Every fall they would visit with a carload of food your mother had canned for us. I know it was a strain on them, too. They had their hands full raising your two brothers. You were lucky to come along after all that, Tess." Rosa saw tears welling up in her sister's eyes and decided to stop.

"No, go on please," Sophie said.

"Well dear, about two years after Frank died, the worst of times happened. There was no steady work to be found and I scrambled from odd job to odd job. I swept floors, did people's laundry and ironing, and even shoveled manure at a horse farm one winter."

The three women chuckled.

"The neighbors and church charities were doing all they could for us. Mel was only five and just starting school. Your uncle Jimmy has always been a hard worker and would do most anything to earn money — mow lawns, rake leaves and that sort of thing. He helped too, but all the while resenting his brother. He always hollered at me if I bought something for Mel. The kid was only a toddler and Jimmy a full five years older. He couldn't understand it completely as an adult would, but he missed his father and I think he considered it Mel's fault that Frank left and never came back."

"But why didn't you give him up?"

Rosa tried to speak again but the words choked in her throat. She looked over to her big sister for help and saw tears streaming down Sophie's cheeks. She had told the story only a few times to her closest of friends, but after all the years it was still hard.

She took a deep breath and continued, "It was a night in February. The weather had been bitterly cold all winter and we were almost penniless. Earlier in the day when the boys were at school, I had telephoned the Social Services office and told the caseworker that I was at the end of my rope and couldn't support both boys anymore. When I told her the situation with Mel not being my child she assured me that she could find a home for him and my life would be better if I let her office intervene. I realized he would most likely end up in a foster home and knew in my heart nobody could care for him like me. Anyway, I was exhausted and agreed. The social worker was scheduled to take custody of Mel the next day after he returned from school."

"Then what happened?" Theresa asked.

"When I went to bed, the reality of it all set in on me. Here was this beautiful little boy about to be turned over to strangers. I had cooked for him, helped him learn to talk, and potty trained him. Who could love him more than me? I began crying in bed and couldn't sleep when I felt this little hand take hold of mine. I looked up and it was little Mel standing by my bed. He told me, 'Don't worry, Mommy, everything will be all right.' He had no idea what was in store for him. I picked him up and put him under the covers with me. I can still feel his cold little feet pressed up against my legs."

"Didn't Jimmy hear you crying, too?" Theresa asked.

"Your uncle Jimmy slept with his bedroom door locked shut and couldn't hear a thing. He always insisted on his privacy. The next morning, after putting the boys on the bus, I called the lady back and told her I couldn't go though with it."

"Now I understand, Aunt Rosa."

"But no, there's more, honey." Rosa saw Sophie wipe the last of her tears. She was smiling now and knew what was coming next.

"That very day I received a letter in the mail from Frank's old boss at the silverware factory. He wrote me that business was improving and that he was hiring back most of the workers like Frank who had been laid off. He offered me my husband's job and I took it. I worked on the assembly line for twenty-two years and earned enough money to support the three of us. When Jimmy's restaurant started doing so well, he bought me a house and I was able to stop working. I even get a small pension now from my years at the plant."

"Mom never told me all of that," Theresa said.

"I know, I asked her not to tell anyone. Even though Mel is not my blood, I will always have a special place in my heart for him. I believe God sent him as an angel to guide me through that miserable time."

Rosa's revelation to her niece was a catharsis and left the women silent. The old glider creaked gently, its sound a comforting match to the cool evening breeze. Sophie was surprised when Rosa kept going.

"You know, Tessy, I've never been able to understand the relationship between Jimmy and Mel either. There were many times when I regretted my decision to keep Mel, not because of the burden, but because of how it affected my own son. I guess sometimes you have to make a choice and then live with it. Those years are a blur to me now. We were just trying to survive."

"You did the best you could, Rosa," said Sophie.

"I know I did, sis, but it saddens me so that the boys have next to nothing to do with each other."

"Well, Mel wrecking Jimmy's car sure didn't help," offered Sophie.

"What?" said Theresa.

As soon as the words left Sophie's outspoken mouth she regretted it. The weight of one more painful memory finally took its toll on Rosa Rosco as she covered her face with both hands trying to hide her tears. Her eyes peeked over at her sister and without saying a word communicated with her that it was OK to finish this final part of the story.

"Tess, before he left for the Navy, Jimmy finished restoring an old car that Frank had been working on when he took off for Georgia. Mel banged it up pretty good."

Rosa nodded to her sister and took over.

"I couldn't get my car started after working a swing shift and the only way I could get home was for Mel to drive Jimmy's car to pick me up. Mel had just gotten his license and the roads were icy. He had an accident on the way."

Without hesitation Theresa interrupted, "But couldn't you have fixed it before Jimmy got back?"

"We did," Rosa answered, "but the paint didn't match up just right and Jimmy could tell the car had been worked on. He swore it never ran right after that. When Mel tried to explain and said, 'Jimmy I'm sorry, but I was only trying to help Mom,' I saw the look on Jimmy's face and was horrified. I've never seen that pained, angry expression since then, but he stood face to face with Mel and simply said, 'She's not your mother.' The coldness in his eyes frightened me."

"What a jerk," Theresa said, "and over a stupid car?"

"That car meant the world to Jimmy," Rosa replied. "The times he spent helping Frank with it in the garage were some of his last memories of his father."

Theresa now felt embarrassed for how quickly she'd rushed to judgment. "Geez, that must have been rough on him."

"Jimmy would sit for hours by himself in that old Ford listening to the radio when he was young. He never forgave Mel. A few weeks after he got home, he lost interest in the thing and sold it."

"What about Mel?" Theresa asked.

"Our little family wasn't the same after that. The relationship between Mel and his brother was pretty much finished. When Mel turned eighteen, he told me it was time for him to leave and he moved out. Without ever saying it, I think he felt guilty about the sacrifices Jimmy and I had made for him. We've never talked openly about it but I know its there, especially now. At times I feel as if he and Rita push me away so that I'll spend more time with Jimmy and his family."

"That's only natural, Rosa. Mel probably does feel odd. He's not your real son and he has his own family now."

"I know, but it still hurts that we've drifted apart. We see each other from time to time and I know he'd be there if I need-ed him, but there's an empty space between us. Maybe its one of those life mysteries that you're never supposed to understand."

Rosa realized for the first time that her niece was holding her hand. She squeezed it softly and looked into her niece's brown eyes.

"When you have kids, you'll understand," she said. Theresa smiled and squeezed back in agreement.

Rosa looked at her watch and saw how late it was. "Whew, I'm beat. It's time for this old lady to go to bed." The women headed back inside to drop off their plates in the sink.

"Get your rest, girls. Tomorrow we weed the garden," announced Sophie.

"Oh, great!" Theresa and her aunt chimed half-heartedly.

Rosa snuggled into bed and gazed at the stars through the open window. She breathed in the fresh air that one can only smell on a farm: a subtle mixture of flowers, vegetable garden, and animals in the barnyard. She hadn't repeated the story about Mel for over twenty years, but after telling it to her niece a calm-ness settled over her. Tonight she felt a strange connection to the boy who had come to her bedside so many years ago. Rosa prayed that both her sons and their families were safe as she drift-ed off to asleep.

She dreamed about making mud pies with her sister when they were kids.

Chapter Ten

Friday night at the Beach was normally an accurate gauge of how business would be for the weekend. It was a beautifully warm evening. The crowd began to flow in, the parking lots filled and people got hungry. Many eventually found their way to the Shack. Mel had three of his best workers on tonight, his stalwarts — Carl and Ron, plus a newcomer named Ollie, whom he had hired last season on Carl's recommendation. The "older guys," as Mel called them, were each eighteen years old and freshly graduated from high school two weeks earlier. None had any intention of going to college.

"A big waste of money," Carl had told his counselor when she encouraged him to apply to some schools after he scored well on a pre-college board exam. The woman saw the teen's potential for further academics despite his mediocre grades and slack attitude. Carl, on the other hand, wasn't interested. He had taken the test on a lark, never dreaming of following through with the real S.A.T. *There are plenty of jobs at the local factories,* he reasoned. Besides, going to college would take him away from his garage and tools.

Working at the Shack five nights a week provided the older guys with money for gas and beer, and the opportunity to meet girls while on the job. Lining up dates from behind the counter was "easy pickings," Ron would say.

The older guys had perfected their night moves and always came up with ways to entertain the ladies: a beach party and bonfire or simply a romantic walk along the waterfront — whatever the choice, the girls seemed to love it. At closing time, there were usually a few young ladies hanging around the Action Corner with a little time left on their curfew clock. They came to the Beach with their families looking to have some fun and the older guys were more than happy to oblige.

Tonight, however, there was work to be done. Even at their young age, Carl, Ron, and Ollie knew how important the holiday weekend was for Mel and his family. The boys hoped it would be profitable, but not just for Mel's sake. Time passed much quicker when things were busy and the sooner they were done, the sooner they could party.

Saturday morning came all too quickly for Mel. When he finally arrived home at 12:30 a.m., he fell into bed without showering or brushing his teeth. A film of cooking grease had accumulated on his face, hands, and arms from the steaming deep fryers. Last night he'd alternated his time between working with the older guys at the Shack and fine-tuning his newly opened arcade next door. He had minimized his start up costs by buying second hand game machines and was still working out their kinks as some jammed or refused to function properly. Despite the hassle of running back and forth between establishments, Mel saw a ray of hope with his investment in the tiny arcade. Automation was the wave of the future and, as he said, "Coin slots are great. The only thing you have to provide the customer is a few laughs." Unlike the food business, with coin operated amusements he didn't have to worry about restocking inventory, spoilage, or a dishonest employee with his hand in the till.

The Shack had done a colossal business last night and Mel was optimistic that the next three days would be the same. God had a way of working miracles, he thought, and great weather coupled with big crowds was just what the Rosco family needed. Mel and Rita had to let their property taxes go delinquent and were three months behind on their mortgage payments. Last night's cash infusion provided the spark Mel needed to get out of bed. He slipped quietly out of the bedroom and let Rita sleep in.

Careful not to wake his family, he made coffee and took his cup with him as he walked across the street toward the lake. His thoughts turned to the incident outside the Shack yesterday with Freddy. Mel hated being the bad guy, but decided he couldn't let the day unfold without giving Carl and Ron a good ass-chewing. He was counting on Rita to smooth things out with Diane.

Morning sunrays cracked through the trees as Mel sat down in a small clearing overlooking the water. Six hours from now this lakeside picnicking spot would be swarming with people having a good time, but right now it offered him a quiet place to think. Mel sipped his coffee and concentrated on Saturday's agenda of restocking supplies and ensuring that his arcade machines worked. As boss, his primary responsibility was to keep things flowing smoothly so his help could work efficiently. No, he didn't carry a clipboard like his brother Jimmy, but he had his own basic, effective way of maintaining records. Notes scribbled on napkins or the palm of his hand seemed to work adequately for him. Mel had a keen way with numbers and was comfortable relying on his memory when dealing with his suppliers. He was a street-smart guy who, despite his other financial missteps, made things happen and usually met his obligations in the end.

Mel cherished these peaceful mornings alone with his coffee, gazing out at the water. His body ached with fatigue but, as he often said to Rita, "We can rest after Labor Day." Donny and Dickie normally didn't work on weekends, as Mel wanted them to enjoy some portion of their summer vacation. This holiday weekend was different, however, and the boys welcomed the idea of making some extra cash and helping the family cause. Sylvia would start her job today making change in the new arcade. Mel welcomed the thought of his daughter working close by, but considered it a mixed blessing. Once the local boys learned of her whereabouts, there'd be a steady stream of suitors eager to get some face time with the young beauty. Mel chuckled to himself, remembering what it was like to be that age. "Hormones with feet" he called the youngsters. Sylvia could be a little on the wild side sometimes, but Mel had confidence that his daughter wouldn't allow socializing to interfere with her job.

The rising sun warmed his face as Mel finished his coffee and headed back home. He thanked the Man Up Above for all that he had. He didn't own a big fancy house on the lake like his brother and he knew he would probably never achieve the financial success Jimmy had obtained. That was OK with him, though. The next few days would be the most important of the season and all he wanted was the chance to make the best of them.

"Hello, Diane, this is Rita." The uncomfortable silence that followed gave Rita a hint of how the conversation was about to go with her sister-in-law.

"Good morning," replied Diane. Her tone confirmed Rita's instincts.

"I'm calling to see how Freddy is doing after what happened yesterday," said Rita.

"Oh, other than being humiliated by his cousin in front of half the town, he's doing just fine. You're lucky I didn't call the police."

"Well, I just wanted you to know that Mel and I are sorry and hope that Freddy didn't hurt himself," Rita said.

"Hurt himself?" shot back Diane. "If those two hoods Carl and Ron acted their age, and your son had any guts, we wouldn't be having this conversation. My poor child is so embarrassed that he hasn't come out of his room all day." Rita knew this was probably true, but then Freddy had no reason to leave his room. The kid had his own television set, a well-stocked fridge, and tons of toys in his bedroom. Other than an occasional trip to the bathroom, Freddy could hole up in there for weeks if he chose to.

"Mel talked to Carl and Ron this morning and they want to apologize and pay for any damages to Freddy's mini bike. As for my son Donald, I don't follow what you're saying."

"You know damn well what I'm saying! What kind of young man stands by idly while his cousin is being persecuted by some bullies? I guess the apple doesn't fall too far from the tree."

With that remark, the patience Rita had so carefully mustered began to fade. She had spent most of the morning rehearsing what she would say, deliberately calling early to catch Diane before she set out to shop or sunbathe. To complicate things further, it was summertime and Diane loved blending up a batch of margaritas or frozen daiquiris at 4:30 every afternoon. By 6:30 she was usually three sheets to the wind and barely cognitive. Rita had a small window of time to iron this out with her or any chance of reconciliation would be lost. She feared the consequences that might result from speaking her mind. Jimmy and Diane were powerful people at the Beach and could make Mel's life harder than it already was.

"Diane, mean-hearted statements like that serve no purpose," Rita said, forcing herself to be composed and still stand firm. "I know that my husband isn't as successful as yours, but he's a decent man. Donny had nothing to do with what happened to Freddy yesterday and I resent what you are saying about my husband and my son."

The phone line went silent. Rita hoped that by staying calm she could appeal to whatever common sense her sister-in-law still had left. Regretfully, her hopes were dashed as Diane spoke in barely a whisper.

"I don't give a shit about you, your stupid children, or your stumble-bum of a husband," she growled through clenched teeth. "You people are pathetic and I'm ashamed to share the same last name. Go to hell, Rita."

Rita stood frozen with nothing but the sound of a dial tone in her ear as Diane hung up.

Freddy Rosco had always been very bright, but channeling that intelligence in a productive direction proved to be near impossible for his parents. He never developed patience or a sense of sharing with his schoolmates. When he joined the Boy Scouts a year ago, Jimmy and Diane thought he'd finally found an activity that interested him. The structure and organization of the Scouts might fill the gaps that were missing in his life.

After the first few meetings Freddy came home excited, eager to develop the rudimentary skills he had learned. Building a lean-to, tying knots, and marching were fun for him. What captivated him most, though, was what he felt by belonging to a group. At the Scout meetings, everything had its place and a sense of order. Tenderfoot through Eagle, everyone belonged. A clear path existed for those willing to learn and work toward a goal.

Diane was so excited for her son, she ran out and bought him a new Scout uniform and every camping gizmo imaginable.

Rather than let Freddy's new life slowly take its own course, as always she chose a path of excess. Soon Freddy became overwhelmed with it all and began acting out toward other troop members. Whatever piece of equipment or tool they had, Freddy had one better and he was eager to show them. When other boys started avoiding him and ridiculing him, he responded with meanness. The Scoutmaster tried to control the situation, but within six months it became apparent that Freddy's behavior was disrupting meetings. For the good of the other boys, the scout leader had to ask Freddy to leave the troop. He called Diane and explained his dilemma: Freddy was a good-hearted kid, but he was just too much for the man to handle and it was taking away from his time with the other boys. Freddy could rejoin the troop in a few months once he learned to get along better with others, the Scoutmaster had told her.

Diane had listened intently and then took the course she normally took when confronted with an unpleasant situation — she attacked the messenger. By the time she was finished with the poor old fellow, he hoped that he never saw Freddy again. In Diane's mind, Freddy's misbehavior was always someone else's fault and her son was a victim. Jimmy was indifferent to the situation and content to let his wife deal with these matters. His job was to run his business and make money, period. After all, Diane was Freddy's mother, he rationalized.

Chapter Eleven

Steve Mills looked like death warmed over. It was 10:15 a.m. and he had missed his 9:30 rendezvous with Donny. Upon seeing Steve cross the street, Donny didn't wait for him to order and simply got his coffee. Steve sauntered over and plunked down on a stool.

"Hey Steve, how you doing?" Donny asked.

Steve took a small sip of coffee and chased it down with a deep drag from an unfiltered cigarette. "OK, Donny, OK," he said softly. He swiveled his stool away from the counter and starred aimlessly out toward the lake. Donny sensed that Steve wanted some privacy this morning. He turned his attention to another customer.

A tall, gray haired gentleman at the other end of the building ordered strawberry ice cream cones for himself and his granddaughter. While scooping, Donny overhead the grandpa saying to the little girl, "Now don't tell your momma or we'll both be in trouble." The girl looked up at the old man, put on a stern face and placed her index finger to her lips: their bond was sealed. The two walked away, hand in hand, giggling as they licked their morning treats. Steve smiled at the two, butted out his cigarette and finally spoke.

"Your dad said you guys had a big night too. We were packed by 9:30 and ran out of Genesee beer by 11. Had to finish the night with nothing but U.C."

U.C. was the nickname for a legendary, cheap local beer, Utica Club. It was well confirmed to produce the best (or worst, depending on one's outlook) hangovers known to man.

"Christ, by that time most of the crowd was so smashed they didn't care," joked Steve. He hacked up some morning crud and started to laugh. A little jolt of caffeine and nicotine was all he needed; the wisecracking saloon guy was himself again.

"Hey Donny, cook me up a couple of dogs and a big order of fries for Willis and Laparco, will ya? I'm gonna serve them breakfast in bed today!"

The two of them laughed as Donny put the order together. Willis and Laparco kept a small room at the Lakeshore down the hall from Steve. After such a busy night Steve let them sleep in, but now it was time for him to crack the whip. Willis needed to fix a leaky sink drain and Laparco had to get on with cleaning out the bar and sorting bottles.

"Any food for you, Steve?" Donny asked as he handed over the eats.

"Naw, maybe later," he mumbled and walked away.

"Rise and shine, boys," Steve belted out. He nudged open the bedroom door with his foot. Steve always referred to Willis and Laparco as his "boys" even though both were grown men. In fact, Willis was three years older than Steve at fifty-nine, but the closeness in age didn't seem to get in the way of their employee/boss relationship.

Steve Mills had never married and at this point in his life didn't have much need for a woman. Over the years, he'd had a few lady friends but his lifestyle was so transient the thought of settling down didn't make much sense. He was happier being a bachelor, independent and unattached. Summers at the Beach with Willis and Laparco were just fine for him.

"What'd you bring us, Steve?" asked Willis. He was already awake but still lying in bed on his side, his head propped up by an arm.

"Coffee, fries, and tube steak," answered Steve. The boys perked up at the smell of food. Hot dogs, hamburgers, and fries were the staple of every carnie and beach rat. It was quick and easy chow that you could grab on the run. Both Willis and Laparco reached over without getting up and dug in.

Steve walked downstairs to his office. Despite the run-down appearance of the old saloon, he prided himself in keeping a neat office and perfect business records. Johnnie Montero, the owner of the joint, was a stickler for keeping the books balanced. After last night's windfall, Steve actually looked forward to tackling the job of sifting through cash register receipts and invoices from vendors. He had locked up the cash last night without counting it, but knew the Lakeshore had a spectacular night. After nearly four decades in the trade, Steve had developed a sixth sense and could usually predict within twenty dollars what the night's take would be. Some evenings the place sent out a certain energy and last night was one of those times. Two more big nights and he was on his way to a nice bonus from Johnnie. Naturally, he would share it with his boys.

"You know, Willis, back at the school we never had hot dogs for breakfast," mused Laparco. "Just stiff oatmeal and hard boiled eggs, that's what we had every morning."

"Sounds pretty boring," replied Willis. Both men were now out of bed and seated at the small restaurant table they'd brought upstairs. It was Willis's idea to place it directly in front of the room's only window, treating them to a beautiful view of the lake while they ate.

"That was sure nice of Steve to bring us breakfast this morning," said Laparco. The hot dogs and fries were a special surprise for them today. Steve liked to eat alone and the two guys fended for themselves, occasionally rummaging through the Lakeshore's kitchen for something to cook, but more often subsisting on the carnival chow that fueled their fellow beach rats. A code of bartering existed at the Beach, as most eateries would comp the local workers or exchange a meal for services. Floors needed to be swept, windows washed, and errands run. Willis and Laparco had mastered the art of trading their ambition and energy for food. Nobody kept score, but things had a way of balancing out. If they were hungry but couldn't find work, merchants normally still offered up a meal, knowing full well that the men would return when needed to square things away. It was a simple, efficient way of doing business. This was the second season that Willis had worked with Anthony Laparco. Steve had kept the introductions brief, but the two men got along well from the start and were slowly learning about one another.

Willis Shank had spent most of his life as a Mr. Fix-it. He'd dropped out of school after the sixth grade, choosing to find a way for himself in the world. He lived a life in and out of foster homes where few adults paid attention to whether or not he went to school. By age fifteen he'd gained a reputation as a natural handyman who had the gift of understanding machinery and building construction. Somebody was always looking for a man with his talents. With the right encouragement Willis probably could have run his own business. Instead, he was more comfortable drifting from job to job on the carnival circuit in the winter, helping out at Montero's bowling alley, and working for Steve at the Lakeshore. This was his nineteenth summer at the Beach.

"See ya downstairs," Willis said. He was already up and dressed.

"OK," Laparco answered with a full mouth. He took his time eating and lingered for a while, savoring the quiet time. Anthony loved this time of day, before the crowds arrived, while the lake's waters were still peaceful. His mind drifted in and out of the life he had left behind.

At twenty-seven years old, Anthony Laparco had spent most of his adult years institutionalized at the New York State School. "The school" was a state-funded home for men and women with emotional or mental problems. Most people referred to it simply as "the nut house." Although Laparco possessed average intelligence, by age twelve it was clear that he wasn't a normal kid. No one in his family could define what "normal" actually was, but Anthony did poorly in school and was unable to fit in with the other kids in his class. His father was in prison and his mother spent her waking hours trying to make ends meet for her five children. As the youngest of the brood, he was doomed from the start. Always last in the pecking order, the effects of disregard rose to the surface in the form of misbehavior. When one of his elementary teachers suggested that he be sent to the State School for rehabilitation, his mother welcomed the idea and considered it the best solution for all concerned.

It was a sad but true fact that many people just like Anthony Laparco, intelligent but neglected human beings, were callously tossed aside by society and sentenced to life in an institution. Nonetheless, even the most hardened counselor at the School could not ignore that this young man was neither mentally retarded nor insane.

Anthony remained at the School for thirteen years. When progressive policies were enacted in the 1960s, many of the residents at the State School were put on trustee programs at local farms and businesses in the area. This was Anthony's second summer at the Beach. He absolutely loved the place and there was not an individual he liked more than Mel Rosco. Whatever the reason, they truly shared a connection. The two of them hit it off from the beginning and both delighted in "busting balls" with each other, as Mel called it.

"Get hot, Laparco!" Mel would shout across the road that separated the Lakeshore and the Shack. This was his way of spurring Laparco to get the lead out and start working.

"Go back to Poland, Mel!" Laparco would holler back, knowing full well that both of them were descended from immigrants and fell in the same melting pot. It was this good natured teasing they looked forward to throughout the season. Willis spent more time with Laparco, but in reality Mel served as the father figure that Anthony never knew. Despite their mutual attraction, however, the two men could not have appeared more different physically. Mel was a medium height, solidly built man with muscular features. He reserved his smiles and frowns for only those closest to him. Laparco, on the other hand, was short and slight in stature except for one glaring feature: his huge round face that bore a perpetual toothy grin. Whether saying hello or goodbye, Laparco's moon-face and teeth jumped out at all those around him. As a child, his comical appearance brought out the worst of human nature. Adults and children made fun of him his entire life, but it was different for him now at Woodland Beach. Maybe it was because the place was full of carnies, misfits, and other strange characters that all got along together trying to make a living; whatever the reason, Anthony Laparco felt at home here.

"Laparco, get down here and give me a hand, will ya?" Willis hollered.

"Sure, Willy, be right there," Laparco answered. He wolfed down the last handful of french fries and got dressed. Time for him to "get hot."

Mel was cashing out Friday night's arcade receipts when Donny called out to him, "Hey Dad, Mom's on the phone." Mel locked the door behind him, grabbed the half-full money bag and crossed the alleyway to the Shack. A pay phone was located on an inside wall by the counter. He grabbed the receiver from his son and sat down.

"Yeah, Rita."

"Mel, it didn't go very well when I called Diane and I'm worried."

"Worried about what?" asked Mel.

"Well," replied Rita, "she had a vengeful tone in her voice. I've given up on having any kind of relationship with her, Jimmy, or Freddy. But I just wanted to let you know that I don't think this is going to go away on its own."

Mel looked at wristwatch: 11:45. Sylvia was scheduled to open up the arcade in fifteen minutes. The last thing he needed this weekend was trouble with his brother. He was struggling to keep himself above water and this Freddy nonsense felt like two cinder blocks tied to his feet.

He took a deep breath and said slowly, "Honey, it's just gonna have to wait. This weekend is too important to us. I know Freddy is capable of making everyone's life miserable and Diane is no help. Jimmy's oblivious and he'll be wrapped up at the Shoreline. We don't have many options here: we have to take care of the present, get the job done, and deal with this Freddy thing later."

"OK, I understand, but I still have a rotten feeling about this." With that, Rita said goodbye and got ready to drive Sylvia to work. The boys usually walked or rode their bikes to work, but Mel insisted that his daughter be chauffeured.

"Let's go, Syl," she called up to her daughter.

Sylvia had spent that last forty-five minutes putting on makeup and brushing her long black hair. "Coming!" she replied. A shot of hair spray, one last-chance look in the mirror and she was on her way.

Chapter Twelve

The weekend forecast called for sunny skies and a high temperature of eighty-one degrees. By noontime, cars were already backed up across the Barge Canal bridge as fun seekers made their way to central New York's summer playground. Donny had done his usual job as the open-up guy. Dickie joined him shortly after, with Carl, Ron, and Ollie at their posts by 11 a.m. Following the respite with his morning coffee, Mel had been on edge all morning long. Rita's phone call about Freddy didn't help his mood, but he actually felt better after lowering the boom on Carl and Ron. It was rare that Carl Wilcox took anyone's criticism without a smart-ass retort, but seeing the stress on his boss's face left him silent. When Mel finished the reaming, Carl responded for both himself and Ron with a meek, "Yes, sir." Satisfied that he had made his point with the two, Mel moved on to more important matters.

Do we have enough stock to handle the crowd today? he asked himself. Worried that he might be short, he had made a run to buy another twenty pounds of hamburger patties. Most of his other supplies were delivered by vendors, but over the years he remained faithful to the local butcher, Rudy Kessler, when it came to his meats. Mel was standing at the door when Rudy opened his shop at 9 a.m.

As the morning progressed, folks started getting hungry and the Shack came to life. The amusement park din continued to build and by three o'clock the place was a swirling mass of lights, sounds, and people.

This was Dickie Rosco's first season "out front," as Mel called it, and he was still learning the routines. In the past, he had been confined to the hot and smelly potato room, the entry level position for workers. The room was nothing more than a small cubicle in the back of the old building. Inside, the rookie on Mel's crew would fill the automatic potato peeler and dice french fries by hand. Jimmy's Shoreline didn't bother with such outdated methods and sold the standard frozen crinkle cut fries like most all the other merchants. Mel, however, prided himself on serving fresh potatoes and customers would line up three and four deep to buy the steaming delights.

Proud to no longer be "bottom man," Dickie happily joined the older boys out front. His replacement, an eleven-year-old named Brucie, was hard at work on the dicer and detached from the activities outside the potato room. Both he and Dickie were oblivious to the ritual that was about to take place.

"Why is Dad carrying all those milkshakes?" Dickie wondered out loud. He saw his father walking back from the Lakeshore with a tray full of tall paper cups.

"Yeah, right, milkshakes," said Carl with a laugh.

"About time, Mel," said Ron. Feigned sarcasm filled his voice.

"I know," Mel replied, fighting back a smile that crept over his face, "but Laparco was chewing my ear off about the bicycle he and Willis found at the dump and rebuilt. He said that he was tired of walking and hitchhiking around and wants his own wheels." Mel lost the battle of trying to contain himself and chortled between words. "I told him to make sure that he got a bike rider's license from the state police or he'd get a ticket. He's hoofing it all the way over to the troopers' barracks right now to get one."

The whole group burst out laughing, knowing that Mel was just busting Laparco's balls. They also knew that, in his own way, Laparco would eventually get even.

Mel doled out the large cups filled with frothy liquid. Everyone but Dickie knew immediately what was really inside. Watching his brother and the older guys attack the drinks, Dickie stared into his cup, and took a big gulp.

"Yuck, this is beer!" the youngster blurted out, his face contorted in disgust.

"Sure is!" Ollie said. On the hottest, busiest days of the season, Mel would sneak the boys ice-cold beer in paper milkshake cups. The older guys were all of drinking age, but for Dickie and Donny, Mel bent the rules a bit. Donny and the others drank theirs, savoring every ounce of the icy brew that the Lakeshore's bartender had comped Mel. This was Mel's quiet way of saying, "Thanks, I know it's hot and you're working hard" to his crew.

"I'll take yours if you don't want it," Ron said.

"Go right ahead! I'll have a Coke," Dickie answered. He wiped the beer foam from his lips and tip of his nose.

There was a lull in business as the crew kicked back for a few more minutes. The lunchtime rush had started around 11 and continued at full bore for nearly four hours as customers roamed the midway or came in from the beach to eat. Mel scrambled to replenish supplies for the boys during the short break. Hot dogs, hamburgers, and fries were flying across the counter today and for the first time in weeks he began to feel the pressure lifting from his shoulders. *Maybe this is our year and my luck has finally turned for the better,* he hoped. Confident that his crew was well stocked for the next wave of eaters, Mel grabbed a beer for himself.

A steady stream of customers lined up for service at Jimmy's Shoreline Inn. Most were either loyal devotees of the establishment or newcomers passing through who had heard of the place from friends. Despite its popularity, the local Beach folk considered Jimmy's food overrated and overpriced. Nonetheless, the Shoreline maintained its reputation as the best spot at the Beach for tourists seeking a decent sit-down meal. Jimmy's waterfront location was prime and his connections with the village tax assessor had allowed him to lower his bottom line, thus giving him a huge advantage over the Beach's other eating establishments. In fact, the Shoreline's annual property taxes were only couple hundred dollars higher than Mel's Shack, even though Jimmy's was four times the size of Mel's tiny place.

When he first took over the restaurant, Jimmy did most of the cooking himself, but with Rosa's help as the business expanded, he was able to attract a talented kitchen staff and his attention was devoted more to managing the operation. Nowadays, he spent most of his time greeting people and overseeing the operation with his clipboard. Customers exchanged pleasantries with him such as "how's the season going?" or "say hi to Diane and Freddy," but Jimmy rarely returned the comments with much more than one-word answers like "thanks" or "OK." He was never known for warmness.

After Mel moved from Rosa's house, years breezed by for the brothers with work and family consuming their time. Routines set in as Jimmy succeeded and Mel floundered. With his business now firmly established, Jimmy's shortcomings were overlooked by most of the community and he and Diane assumed a prominent status in town. His ownership of a landmark restaurant, coupled with his rising financial prowess, wiped the slate clean of his previous reputation of aloofness. Village sycophants sprang to his aid now. This holiday weekend, Jimmy had the luxury of not looking down the barrel of a financial gun like his younger brother did. For him it was business as usual — "parties of four or less" in one line, "parties of five or more" in another.

Chapter Thirteen

Before the Shack's crew knew it, the time was 6 p.m. The pace had been so fast that none of the five boys paid much attention to the clock. Sylvia was relieved by a guy Mel had hired shortly after opening the arcade. Bob was a forty-one-year-old school teacher who welcomed the chance to make extra money between June and September. He'd spent the last two summers roofing houses. This new gig making change and overseeing the arcade felt like being on vacation compared to swinging a hammer and carrying shingles up a ladder.

"OK, Donny and Dickie, you guys can knock off," said Mel. It was a good thing for Dickie. The heat was getting to him and the little guy was ready to call it a day. Mel put on a fresh apron and prepared to join the three older guys to finish up the rest of the night. Throughout the day he had bounced back and forth between the Shack and the arcade, handling crises as they occurred. A couple of pinball machines kept jamming up, causing customers to get frustrated and take their business elsewhere. Mel had answered Sylvia's pleas for help a half dozen times to come free up coin mechanisms and keep the cash flowing. Also, young Brucie's mother only allowed her son to work for three hours so Mel had filled in at the potato room as well. Surprisingly, despite the constant running between businesses, he felt great. The rapid tempo coupled with the promise of another flush day kept his adrenaline going.

Dickie tossed his apron in the dirty linen bin and was out the door when Mel noticed that Donny was still wearing his.

"Dad, can I work the night shift with you guys?" he asked. Mel had allowed his eldest son to work after dark a few times but never on a Fourth of July weekend. The Beach became rowdy at night and with the throngs pouring in, the combination of heat, crowded streets, and boozed up vacationers usually meant an atmosphere for trouble. Mel didn't want his kids to be around that.

"Are you sure you don't want to call it a day?" asked Mel.

"Dad, I feel OK and the way business is going you could use an extra hand." Mel knew Donny was probably right and realized his son understood how critical this weekend was to the family. Customers would wait in line for food only so long until they moved on to the next establishment. Having Donny onboard for the night shift would enable the Shack to pump out orders at a maximum rate.

"OK pal, you stay on until nine o'clock and we'll see how it goes from there."

Sylvia was already in the front seat when Rita pulled her station wagon up to the Shack. She handed Dickie a large box and motioned for him to carry it back to the crew. Inside was a pan of lasagna with paper plates and utensils. The older guys loved Rita's cooking and showered her with thanks as they tore into it, shoveling down bites between customers. Despite being surrounded by food, they grew tired of seeing and smelling the same stuff and ate very little during the day.

Rita accepted the thank-yous with a wave and a smile. She drove off slowly, carefully dodging the mob hovering around the Action Corner.

Freddy Rosco sat alone in his air-conditioned bedroom. He could hear the busy traffic on Main Street and the clanking music sounds of the amusement park down the road. It was a warm, sunny day and, by all that was right, he should have been outside playing in the park or at the beach. He chose instead to sit at home and mope. After the mini bike incident yesterday, his mother and father had both spoken to him, but separately. When asked what responsibility he had, he denied any wrongdoing and portrayed himself as the innocent victim.

Jimmy said to him, "Freddy, those guys wouldn't have thrown water on you for no reason. What did you do?"

"Nothing!" Freddy shouted back. "They're just jealous because I have nice things and they don't." Jimmy suspected that there was more to the story, but he didn't have time to pursue it. It was dinner hour, the busiest time of the day, and his thoughts had already shifted back to the restaurant.

The Shoreline was well staffed and he left no detail to chance in planning for the weekend. Still, he felt obliged to get back to work and left Freddy by himself again. Diane, on the other hand, reacted differently. Refusing to even consider that there might be two sides to Freddy's story, she had charged ahead on a verbal tirade condemning Mel Rosco's family and the delinquents who worked for him at the Shack. Freddy quietly glowed inside, knowing that he had duped both Jimmy and Diane into thinking he had been casually riding by his uncle's business when all hell broke loose. He knew that his parents possessed neither the time nor the desire to drill him for the facts. Freddy alienated just about everybody he encountered at the Beach and he liked it that way. By doing so, he never had to extend himself or please any-one. He ruled his own little kingdom. It was summer vacation and with no school to attend, life was simple: eat, sleep and live in the world according to Freddy.

Bored again, he made himself a sandwich and turned on the TV. The first show he dialed was an episode of *The Three Stooges*. Great, he thought. He could waste away another hour doing exactly what he wanted: nothing. Anyway, he figured he would need his energy for later.

By 8:45 it was clear that this was a special night at Woodland Beach. Steve and Mel passed briefly on the street between the two businesses and agreed that neither of them had ever seen such a crowd of people. The public lot by the Lakeshore was jammed and cars were backed up over the bridge and down the highway for over a mile. There were no more open parking spots left in town so people resorted to parking their vehicles on strangers' lawns, in alleys, or wherever they could find an opening. It was the perfect summer night to be in business at the Beach. Mel's crew had already gone through all the diced potatoes Brucie had prepared earlier and Mel filled in again as the potato guy. On a night like this he felt most useful helping the other guys as need-ed. He owned the place but wasn't afraid to get his hands dirty. His employees respected this and seeing Mel getting just as sweaty and dirty as them was a catalyst to work harder.

"Blanch 'em!" barked out Ron. This was the signal for who-ever had a free hand, usually the potato guy, to scoop up raw, diced fries and load them into two large metal baskets. The pota-toes were then lowered into a large vat of hot peanut oil to pre-cook. After a few moments, the fry guy would test for proper blanching by raising a basket from the oil and squeezing a fry with his fingers. If he did this too slowly he'd burn his fingers. It took some practice, but Ron had mastered the art without covering his hands with blisters. When the fries were cooked enough to easily squeeze in half, they were blanched and ready for the next step: finish frying. The blanched spuds were OK to sit in that half-cooked state for an hour or so before finish frying and on a slow day that's just what happened. Not now, however. Tonight there was a continuous cycle from the potato peeler to dicing, blanching, and finish frying. Mel and his crew were in effect converting bags of raw potatoes to cash that would feed and clothe his family and pay his bills.

Carl was on the grill, Ron on the fryers, Ollie ran drinks, popcorn, and ice cream at the far end of the building, and Donny stood between Ron and Carl taking orders and making change. The arrangement was an uncomplicated but efficient way to run the establishment. No complex procedures, detailed instructions, or fancy uniforms. Not rocket science but it worked.

Scooping up more fries for blanching, Mel looked up at Donny.

"You all right to keep working, Donny?" he asked. He knew the answer before his son gave it but he felt he had to ask anyway.

"Yup," Donny replied with a defiant grin.

"OK, pal, then you're here until closing tonight," Mel said, not looking up as he nodded to Ron who lowered another ten pounds of potatoes into the bubbling oil.

"*Well*, Mr. D. gets to break curfew for a change, huh?" teased Carl. "Good, we're gonna need you." He emptied a box of two dozen hot dogs onto the grill. The next three hours passed like no time at all. Mel thought briefly about making another "milkshake" run but decided against it when Bob flagged him down to help repair another jammed pinball machine.

"Mel, you're going to have to pay me a bonus or I'm going to back to roofing," joked Bob. He wiped his brow with the back of his hand as the two of them walked briskly to the arcade. Mel notice Bob was sweating through the short sleeve dress shirt he wore. "I never would've guessed I'd be up and down on my feet so much in that little building."

"I warned you what it's like here over a Fourth weekend," Mel replied. "I've been here all my life and never seen business like this before. My wife prayed a rosary this morning for a good day, but this unreal."

"Can she say a rosary for my sore feet tomorrow morning?" pleaded Bob. Both men laughed as Mel sorted through the wad of keys dangling from his hip to unlock the machine.

Across the street, the Lakeshore Hotel was rocking, literally. Steve hired bands for Friday and Saturday nights and, this being a Golden Weekend, did so for Sunday as well. There were three other joints within two hundred yards of the Shack, all with live music tonight. Since the Lakeshore was the closest, the sounds of Billy Ray and the Upbeats was the music that came through the clearest to Mel's crew, carrying over the rest of the noise. Billy Ray led a four-man guitar band that played everything from Elvis to British rock with some Motown songs thrown in by request. The place was packed with a long line of partiers outside waiting to get in. The doorman at the Lakeshore was a heavy-set man named Ralphie, who sat on a stool tapping his feet and checking IDs. When the spirit really moved him, he hopped off his perch and broke out in a solo dance. Tonight was one of those nights and upon seeing the rotund guy gyrating, Mel and his crew stopped to watch. "Go, Ralphie, go!" they chanted. He waved back and his smile said it all; it was another terrific night for the Lakeshore too.

By the time 12:15 rolled around, Mel and his crew were thankful that business was tapering off and people were heading home. He gave the order to wrap it up and the crew started putting away food and powering down equipment. Carl began the job of scraping the grills clean but Mel took over the job from him. Nobody cleaned a grill like Mel. Sweat dripped lightly from his forehead as his short, thick arms stroked back and forth with the black grill stone in hand. When he was done, he could almost see his reflection in the polished iron. Carl, Ron, Ollie, and Donny finished their duties in about fifteen minutes and tossed their dirty aprons into the clothes bin. The three older guys had lined up dates with some girls earlier and planned to meet them at a late night beach party that would most likely last until dawn. They started busting balls over who would go after which girl when Mel said, "Hey guys, here." He handed them each a ten dollar bill. Payday was Monday but his crew deserved a bonus tonight. He turned to Donny and shook his hand with an extra firm grip. Mel didn't speak to his oldest child, but simply beamed a proud smile that a father reserves only for his children. When their hands separated, Donny saw a ten dollar bill in his palm as well.

Mel cashed out the register, not bothering to count the day's take. He could tell pretty much what kind of night they'd had just by the weight and volume of the two sacks. Bob had already cashed out the arcade and Mel was pleased with the first Saturday night's receipts from his new venture. He was the last one out of the building. The older guys were well on their way to the party scene. He and Donny had walked a dozen steps toward the truck when Mel said, "Donny, I'm not sure Ron turned off all the fryers. We need to check them."

"Give me the keys and I'll do it, Dad. You can get the truck and meet me out front."

"OK, will do," answered Mel, anxious to go home and get some rest. "Make sure the red lights are out over each of the three fryer control knobs. That's how I double check that the power is off." This was the first time that Donny had stayed at work until closing time. He scooted back to the Shack, unlocked the door, and peeked around the corner to the fryers. No red lights.

"Yeah, they're off," he called out to Mel as he closed the door again and secured the padlock, giving it a firm tug to ensure it was set. Mel swung the truck out of the parking lot as Donny jogged about twenty yards to meet him and hopped in. Mel slowed the truck to a crawl as they cruised by the building; he and his son stared at the old place for a few seconds. It had been a long, tiring day for both of them. Donny started to feel fatigue as the night's excitement wore off. Mel pressed the accelerator down and they sped away. Exhausted, neither said a word on the way home.

When Mel and Donny arrived, Rita and Sylvia were still up and seated at the kitchen table.

"What are you girls doing up so late?" Mel asked as he plunked down the money bags on the counter.

"Just chatting," answered Rita, looking over a cup of hot chocolate she had made for herself and Sylvia. Mel realized that he and Donny had most likely interrupted a private conversation between mother and daughter. With Dickie sound asleep by 9:30, the two women had spent the last several hours talking about things only they could share — clothes, men, local gossip, and menstrual cycles.

"Well, we had a pretty good night," Mel said. "Donny here put in a fifteen hour day and we all deserve to sleep in tomorrow." Donny's normal open-up routine would slide to noon.

Even the campers and partiers took time off on Sunday morning. Mel and the family would do the same.

"Good night," the men said as they shuffled upstairs.

Sylvia and her mom maintained a close, open relationship. At sixteen years old, Sylvia was comfortable talking with her mother about most topics, even sexual issues, but Rita knew that there were some boundaries, and she was savvy enough to avoid them rather than embarrassing the girl. The universal attraction between boys and girls was a natural thing and Rita did her best to keep a cool head when the boys came around. She did a better job of it than her husband. When Sylvia had received her first phone call from a male suitor at age twelve, Mel blurted out, "She's too young for this!" Rita calmly put his fears to rest, impressing on him that it would be better to go with the flow and neither encourage or discourage the harmless courting.

"What was on your mind at that age?" Rita had asked her husband. She smiled while waiting for his response.

"Yeah, I guess you're right," Mel answered sheepishly. Sylvia was developing a rather serious relationship with John and, in her own gentle way, her mother wanted to learn in what direction it was headed. Sylvia assured her mom that both she and John were behaving themselves and yes, she was still a virgin. Rita was a little stunned to hear the words from Syl, but both women seemed relieved to finally get that fact out in the open. That was the topic that led to the hours of chatting that had just transpired. With that news off the table, their conversation had taken many paths that diverged, converged, and prompted laughter and some tears from both of them. Rita explained the basics of the family's financial problems and Sylvia listened intently. Like many firstborn, she had a slightly different bond with her parents when it came to adult matters like family problems and money.

"Wow, it's 1:30. We'd better hit the sack, young lady," Rita stood up and stretched her arms over her head.

"I love you, Mom," Sylvia said softly and gave her mother an extended hug.

"I love you too, Sylly girl," replied Rita. She cherished moments like this and knew that there would be fewer and fewer of them as time marched on. They walked upstairs quietly, taking care to not disturb their men. As they passed the boys' bedroom they laughed at Dickie's snoring.

Chapter Fourteen

Ollie closed the car's trunk with his elbow; his hands were filled with beer cans Carl had iced down on the way to work. His friend always kept a cooler in the trunk, along with a couple of old blankets. The blankets came in handy when he crawled under the car to make unexpected repairs and to protect the Buick's finish when he leaned on a fender, working under the hood. Tonight, however, the blankets were destined to be used by him, his two buddies, and some cuties on the beach sand. The blankets and cooler joined Carl's other "emergency" supplies in the trunk: a tool box, jumper cables, extra motor oil, road flares, and a shop manual. Carl's parents had once told him that if he put as much thought into his schoolwork as he did into his car, he'd be an honor student. They were probably right: the young grease monkey kept a respectable B grade average with virtually no time spent studying. His passion was automobiles, and everything in his life revolved around them.

"Come on, let's go!" Carl hollered as Ollie handed him the keys and slid into the back seat. As he sat down, he lost his grip

85

on the wet cans; they fell in his lap and then rolled onto the car seat.

"Hey, be careful, don't sit on our . . ."

"Yeah, I got it Ron, don't sit on your clothes," Ollie answered sarcastically. He was worn out and so was Ron. Mel's generosity had lifted the boys' spirits but after twelve hours of work they were edgy.

"Here, Ron, maybe this will cool you down." Ollie pulled out an opener, punched two holes in the can, and handed it to his pal. He did the same for himself and Carl, who was negotiating his way through the crowded parking lot. The last of the diehards were finding their cars and heading home from a night at the amusement park. The time was just past 12:30 and the rides and eateries were all closed. The joints shut their doors a little later at 1 a.m., with last call going down at 12:45. There was a steady flow of people emptying from the Lakeshore and other bars, all convening on the lot at the same time and creating a small traffic jam. Carl placed the beer between his legs and tapped his horn in hopes of clearing a path out for him to turn onto Park Avenue. A couple of drunks were directly in front of the car, nose to nose, hollering about something. Carl revved the engine and honked again. They scattered, slipped him the finger, and stumbled off arm in arm, laughing.

"Don't bother, Ron, they're shit-faced," Carl said to his buddy, who was halfway out the car door headed toward the derelicts. Of the three, Ron had the shortest fuse, and it didn't take much urging for him to lock horns when crossed. Known around town as a fierce street fighter, he bruised his knuckles on heads for less provocation then being flipped the bird.

"It's not worth it, man, get back in," Carl pleaded to his friend. "We already pissed off Mel with that Freddy thing the other day. All you gotta do now is get arrested again and miss work tomorrow." Ron relented, sat back and chugged the rest of his beer. He looked over at his friend and nodded that he understood. Earlier in the evening, during a happier moment, he'd schmoozed three girls from Utica who were spending a week at the lake with their sorority sisters. The girls lingered by the french fry counter for over twenty minutes, attracted to Ron's long hair, blue eyes, and welcoming smile. He made polite small talk with the ladies, never breaking from his job on the fryers. Finally, one of the teens got up enough courage to invite him and his two buddies to a party at their sorority's camp on the north shore.

"Step on it, Carl, we gotta get cleaned up and head over there before someone else moves in on those chicks." Ollie tossed his empty can on the floor and instinctively opened another. He'd been eyeing the girls from across the Shack as they flirted with Ron. There was a tall, skinny brunette, a short brown-haired girl with big breasts, and the third, a quiet nondescript one whose mop of hair shrouded her face and made it difficult to judge her looks.

Ollie put his nose to his armpit and announced, "Man, I'm gross." Carl and Ron performed the same self-test and agreed. It was blind luck that Ollie lived on the way to the sorority camp; the boys wanted to shower and change into fresh clothes.

The Buick's big engine idled gently as Carl switched off the car's headlights and eased into the driveway. Other than the screeching of crickets, the place was silent. The boys tried to be quiet, but the pending excitement overcame them and the more they struggled to contain their giggles, the louder they got.

"Knock it off or you'll wake my parents," Ollie whispered. "Stay here, I'll get some soap and towels." He opened the back porch's screen door and went inside. Carl turned on the shower Ollie's dad had rigged up at his wife's request; Ollie and his father were avid fishermen, loved to water ski, and were on the lake whenever they had free time. The outdoor sink and shower gave them a spot to clean their catch and wash up without tracking a mess into the house.

"Smells like someone went fishing today," Carl said, referring to the stray fish guts left in the sink. He let out a sigh when the shower's warm spray hit his skin. Ollie tossed him a bar of soap and he started scrubbing vigorously. Carl's skinny, untanned body glistened in the dim light. Unlike his buddies, he despised the summer sun and rarely went swimming. His childhood nickname was "Whitie."

"Yeah, we had a good day; caught the limit by 10 this morning," Ollie answered. Carl moved over and dried off as Ron hopped under the water for his turn.

The three boys took no longer than five minutes total to shower down; it felt great to get the grease and sweat off their skin, a refreshing energizer after a long, hot day of work. The two cans of beer they had each chugged on the drive, together with the warm shower, set them in a good mood and ready to party. Ollie tossed the wet towels and his dirty clothes onto the porch. As he climbed into the back seat he was overwhelmed by the sweet smell of Canoe aftershave.

"You guys got anymore of that?" he asked. Ron obliged, grabbed the small glass bottle from the glove compartment, and tossed it back to Ollie.

"Well, we're clean, wearing fresh clothes and we smell like French whores, so maybe one of us will get lucky tonight." Ollie said. The radio blared out a song by the Beach Boys. The three sang along to their favorite group and busted balls over who'd get the small girl with the big breasts. Ollie insisted it should be him since he was the shortest of the three.

Carl parked on the grass in front of the sorority's cottage. It was already 1:30 but the party was still going; chatter and laughter filtered out from the beach where everyone was gathered around a fire.

Mel's crew found the girls and were greeted by enthusiastic waves when the ladies recognized them; they hadn't yet paired off with any boys. Seeing this, Carl, Ron, and Ollie scanned the campfire and smiled at one and other.

Ollie raided the cooler again, discreetly carrying six beers down to the waterfront. The girls grabbed the cans before he had a chance to offer. They looked over their shoulder toward the cottage and then around the rest of the group. Nobody seemed to be watching, so they held the cans up for Ollie to open. Alcohol was prohibited during sorority week at the lake, although it was common knowledge amongst the parents and chaperones that the rule was near impossible to enforce; teens always found a way to sneak a drink if they really wanted to. Provided none of the girls got sick or in trouble, the adults generally turned their heads to what they knew was a rite of passage into adulthood for the girls.

The cold brew mellowed everyone and the group's conversation lulled into soft talk as boys and girls paired off: Carl with the tall, skinny brunette, Ron with the quiet one, and Ollie sat next to the short girl with the large chest. Carl looked over toward Ollie and his date and raised his beer in a mock salute as if to say "well done."

Ron used all of his charms to get the quiet one to come out of her shell, seeing that behind that mane of hair was a pretty face. Like him, she had steel blue eyes. He whispered something in her ear, she laughed heartily, shook her head, and began telling him a story about something.

Content that his pals were doing OK on their own, Carl turned his attention to the thin brunette sitting at his side; she smiled warmly and without saying a word conveyed she was glad to be with him tonight.

Teens pulled their blankets around them and edged closer to the fire as the day's heat gave way to a cool, damp breeze off the water. The laughter and banter wound down as they began hugging and kissing.

Chapter Fifteen

"Laparco, wake up, wake up!" Anthony Laparco opened his eyes to see Willis standing over him. Moonlight cast a ghoulish glow on his roommate's face.

"Is it time to get up?" He rubbed his eyes groggily.

"No, damn it, it's 2:30 in the morning and you're having another bad dream," Willis said.

"Oh, sorry," said Laparco. He took a deep breath and sat up. The psychologists called them night terrors. He seldom remembered the dreams after he woke up, but this had been a particularly scary one and he recalled it vividly. He was being chased by someone carrying a knife while running naked in a field outside the State School. He was drenched in sweat and breathing heavily. Steve Mills had asked Willis to share a room with Laparco when he first came on board at the Lakeshore, primarily to watch over the guy and make sure he didn't cause any problems. After his first season, the two decided to keep the roommate arrangement, neither one of them looking forward to being alone at night in the creaking old structure. Having another person close by was usually all that Anthony Laparco needed to feel safe.

Once he was asleep, however, his mind wandered wherever it wanted to go.

"I think I'll go outside for a while and get some air."

Willis slurred something that sounded like "good idea" and was back to snoring within seconds of his bald head hitting the pillow. Laparco groped in the darkness for some clothes, got dressed, and left the room. He tiptoed down the narrow hallway, descended the stairs, and went out the hotel's side door. Just being outside helped him center his thoughts: the sound of surf and the evening's light breeze had a soothing affect. Nighttime was the worst for him. Normally, Willis was more understanding, but the old fellow was exhausted and grumpy. He'd been working like a dog all week and there were still two more long days to go this holiday weekend.

Anthony walked slowly across the street by the Shack and then turned toward the parking lot that led to the water. Not a soul was around. The amusements, concessions, and joints were locked tight and it was still a couple of hours before even the most eager fishermen would arrive to wet their lines.

Calmer now, Laparco thought how lucky he was to be out of the School and leading a better life here at the Beach. Willis, Steve, Mel and his crew were close to his heart and he didn't want Labor Day to arrive, signaling the season's end. His seemingly permanent grin turned up an added notch as he continued his walk around the backside of Mel's arcade. Earlier in the week, Mel had handed him a roll of quarters and invited him to test out the arcade games. He spent two hours playing until Willis came in and dragged him back to work.

When he first came to the Lakeshore, Anthony Laparco was a different man. Having spent most of his formative years in an institution, he wasn't prepared for the new freedoms he had on the outside. His counselors realized early on that he possessed more intelligence than most all of the other patients. But being sheltered from the world outside the School, he never experienced the twists and turns that life offers up. His world was regimented behind the walls and he felt safer with it that way. No need to set an alarm clock; bells rang every morning at 6:15 signaling a new day. Breakfast, lunch, and dinner were prepared for him. Lights out at 10 p.m. Even recreation time was planned. When he was released for a trial period to work at Johnnie Montero's bowling alley, Anthony Laparco was lost. His newfound friend, Willis Shank, tried steering him in the right direction but it was a long haul for both of them. Anthony became agitated for the simplest reasons and missed the security of life at the School. When Montero asked him to spend a couple more weeks helping Willis at his other business, his initial response was no. He'd never been there and change did not appear to be his friend. The day he stepped out of Montero's sedan at the Beach, he acted like a frightened animal. He literally cowered when passersby approached him.

Mel Rosco was the first person at the Beach to befriend him. More out of sympathy than good will, he invited Willis and Laparco into his home for dinner one evening. Willis had known Mel and his family for years and felt at ease in their house. Laparco, on the other hand, sat silently at the table, trying his best to be comfortable but failing miserably. Rita graciously struck up a conversation with him but it was like talking to a four-year-old. Despite his age of twenty-five, Laparco had no social skills. Sylvia, Donny and Dickie looked on with confusion and pity. *What's wrong with this guy?* they thought.

Throughout the meal Rita unconsciously refilled his glass with lemonade and Laparco obligingly continued to drain it. At the State School, patients were required to clean their plates and empty their glasses. His plate of lasagna had long since disappeared but he was struggling to keep his glass empty. After a half dozen refills he finally blurted out, "May I go to the bathroom, please?" The mealtime conversation came to a halt. Laughing gently, Rita answered, "Sure, Anthony," and pointed to the bathroom door. Dickie choked back laughter as Laparco bolted from his chair, slammed the bathroom door closed and proceeded with a loud, forty-five-second long urination. He returned to the table red-faced but relieved. When Rita leaned toward him and asked, "Better?" he nodded his head and beamed a wide grin that exposed his front teeth. Ever since that day Anthony Laparco had found a special place in the hearts of Rita, Mel, and their children. His cross-street banter with Mel became as much a part of the midway's landscape as the grinding and buzzing of the Bomber ride. Over the following two years, Anthony Laparco came out of his shell, found some joy, and lived the way God intended for him.

As he continued his walk around Mel's property something startled him: a flash of light from somewhere lit up the darkness. At first he thought it was an approaching car, but when it got brighter, he saw that it was coming from the Shack's second floor windows.

Why is someone up there at this hour? he thought. Mel sometimes used the small loft to store paper goods, both other than that the space went unused. As he got closer he smelled something burning. Gray smoke seeped out from the Shack's wooden shutters. Looking up, he could now see flames lapping against the window panes. The word "fire" froze in his mouth. He tried, but couldn't get his lips to move, and when he did, the sound was more of a croak than a discernable word. After a few seconds, he got control of himself and ran back to the Lakeshore to rouse Steve and Willis. Laparco frantically searched his pockets for a key but came up empty. In his bleariness while getting dressed, he'd forgotten to take it and the door locked behind him when he walked out.

He pounded on the door, but soon realized that Steve and Willis were sleeping at the other end of the building and probably couldn't hear him. *My bike! I could ride my bike for help,* he thought. But no, worried that someone might steal it, he always kept it locked in the storeroom at night. Panicked now, his mind scrambled for what to do. The firehouse was a half mile away on Main Street. His only chance of getting help was to run the distance and pull the alarm handle outside the building.

Convinced that this was his only option, he tore off running through the park, but stumbled to the ground after a few steps. In the darkness he hadn't been able to find his sneakers and had slipped on the first thing he grabbed, his shower shoes. He got to his feet, kicked them off but fell again, this time tripping over a fallen tree branch. Emotions overcame him as he started to sob in frustration. He bent over, resting his hands on his knees, and looked at the Shack. Light from the growing flames now illuminated the trees and surrounding buildings. *I can't stop now! I'm the only one who can help!* Without hesitation, he got up again and bolted from the park's darkness and onto Main Street. The hard pavement hurt his bare feet but he pressed on. He saw a lone car in the distance, waved his arms and screamed out, "help!" but the driver turned onto a side street and disappeared.

Laparco remembered the Olympic runners he'd seen on TV. It looked so easy for them and they ran so fast. He pumped his arms like they did but he felt like he was moving in slow motion. In his entire life, he'd never run much farther than the distance from home plate to first base and this was a strange sensation: he didn't understand why his legs were cramping up. His pace slowed to barely a jog but he refused to give in and walk. He could see the big firehouse now. Only a couple of hundred yards to go! The alarm box stood out brightly, a red light shining above it. Almost there! Fifty, forty, thirty yards. Why were his legs so heavy?

Swoosh! A bicycle went flying past him, its rider pedaling furiously. Laparco kept going but his eyes followed the bike as it made a sharp right turn and faded out of view. He didn't see the rider's face but something looked familiar about the fancy bike. As he turned his head back around, he jerked to a stop, nearly slamming into one of the big firehouse doors. Covered in sweat and barely able to stand now, he lunged at the alarm box and pulled down the lever. After a short pause, the siren kicked in, winding up slowly to a deafening howl.

Totally spent, he crumpled to the ground and covered his ears. His legs were throbbing and the bottoms of his feet burned.

The siren cut through the night air, finding its way to the eardrums of sleeping firefighters. Most were in bed with wives or girlfriends. Many had been out drinking at beach parties or bars. Reality edged out slumber as the men sat up, placed their feet on the floor, and prepared for duty. With the exception of Chief Al Johnson and two deputies, no one received a dime for their service. They came from all walks of life — grocery clerks, mechanics, unemployed handymen, and even one physician. The men had one thing in common, though, and that was a strong sense of obligation to their community.

As usual, Chief Al would be the first to arrive at the firehouse. A special hot line was rigged at his house to ring whenever the fire whistle was tripped. After years of practice, Al was dressed and on his way in less than two minutes. A factory foreman by trade, he'd held the position of fire chief for the last six years. For his efforts he was paid two hundred dollars per year and had use of the station-owned pickup truck. The road was empty ahead so Chief Al decided to turn on the truck's flashing beacon but left the siren off. No need to make any more noise, he thought; the siren woke up everyone within five miles.

He pulled into the empty lot and parked in his reserved spot. The siren continued to wail but it didn't bother him. After decades working in a loud factory and scores of fires, Al figured he was probably half deaf by now.

"Where's the fire, Al?" called out another fighter who pulled in after him.

"Don't know. Just got here myself," Al replied with his trademark brevity.

"The Shack's on fire. I . . . I . . . I pulled the alarm," Laparco said. Chief Al jumped back: he never saw Laparco in the shadows.

"Who the hell are you?" demanded the chief.

"I was taking a walk and saw fire and smoke so I ran down here to pull the lever," Laparco said, still sitting underneath the alarm box. His ankles ached as he rubbed them, hoping to ease the pain. A few more men arrived and raised the station's doors. Hearing Laparco's words, one of them turned in the direction of the amusement park and said, "Holy shit, that place is a tinder box!" A faint but steady glow could be seen flickering over the midway.

"Looks like he's right," Johnson said. Calmly, he turned back toward the station and started barking orders, much like a seasoned submarine captain would when preparing to dive. Lights came on, doors slammed open and closed as men scattered in all directions carrying out their designated tasks. Laparco stood up and got out of the way as more and more men bee-lined into the station.

A gaggle of volunteers hopped on the first truck as it lumbered out the door. Laparco stood to the side and watched the dizzying display of sound, motion, and lights. A second truck rolled onto Main Street and roared off. Its mission fulfilled, the fire whistle was switched off and wound down. Hubbub at the station ceased as the noise and action shifted to the fire scene.

Cars raced by, house lights came on, and citizens peered out their windows at the disruption. A stream of pedestrians made their way down Main Street to watch the excitement. One firefighter stayed behind and was shouting something into a walkie-talkie. Laparco found himself being drawn from the empty firehouse into the throng headed toward the fire. He limped but kept pace with the crowd. In the distance he saw flames leaping above the treetops now. A second wind came over him and he started a slow jog. Surprisingly, the movement made his legs feel better.

Chapter Sixteen

Carl pulled at the blanket in an attempt to cover himself; the damp, humid air was cold now. He swatted away a mosquito buzzing around his head. His neck hurt as he sat up and looked around: Ron and Ollie were passed out, the campfire had burned down, and everyone else had left the beach party. The night had been fun, although too short. The three girls had all headed back up to the sorority camp before anything serious could develop between him and his new acquaintance. Her name was Beverly and she had asked him to call her soon. Carl struggled to remember her number, but couldn't. God, he was tired! The beers and long work day had finally caught up with him. He thought of waking Ron and Carl and driving home, but figured it must be close to daybreak so he might as well let them be. He stared at his watch but couldn't focus his eyes enough to read the time, so he curled up and drifted back to sleep. He thought he was dreaming when he heard the muted sound of a fire whistle.

Late night sirens were a common occurrence at the Beach, especially on a Saturday night during the season. Rowdy beach parties, heavy drinking, and an overall reckless population often led to distress in the small community. Car accidents, fires, and other emergencies increased on the weekends when the village populace grew in size.

One of the more bizarre events had happened three summers ago when a camper from Binghamton decided to chain saw a tree next to his cottage after midnight. Neighbors called the police to complain, but while en route to the scene, the patrol officer received word that an ambulance was also dispatched. The tree fell in the opposite direction that the drunken lumberjack had intended, landing squarely on his cottage and pinning his wife in their bedroom. The firehouse siren was activated to call out a rescue team. Miraculously, the woman survived, suffering only a broken arm after being trapped between the tree trunk and a dresser. Saturday night sirens were part of the Beach's heritage and most non-firefighters found a way to ignore them and go back to sleep.

Mel Rosco had just dozed off after being awakened by the siren. When the phone rang, Rita instinctively picked up the receiver and handed it across the bed to her husband.

"Yeah."

"Mel, it's the Shack," said Steve, out of breath. Mel didn't bother to reply. He bolted out of bed and threw on the first set of clothes he could find. Rita was up with him. She had heard Steve's gravely voice as Mel held the receiver loosely against his ear. She turned on a light and raced to get dressed.

Sylvia was the first one at their bedroom door. "What's the matter, Mom?" she asked timidly.

"The Shack is on fire," Rita answered. She didn't look up at her daughter. Sylvia was speechless. She stood frozen in her parents' bedroom doorway as they brushed by her and down the hallway. Donny and Dickie were awake, but still in the room they shared. They had heard their mother's words to their sister and sat up.

"Dad?" Donny called as Mel and Rita rushed down the stairs. His father didn't answer.

"Sylvia, stay here with your brothers, please," said Rita. The sternness in her voice startled her daughter. She had never heard her mother speak like this.

"OK, Mom," Sylvia answered, fighting back tears.

Mel had the truck started and in front of the house by the time Rita came out. As they rounded the corner onto Main Street the glow of the blaze filled their view.

The first faces they recognized through the smoke were those of Steve, Willis, and Laparco. The three men were working fervently to save the amusement games Mel had accumulated in his budding arcade. Steve grabbed one of the firefighters and convinced him to bash in one of the arcade's overhead doors. Only twenty feet separated the arcade from the burning Shack. Steve figured there was a good chance the flames might spread and destroy both buildings. The three men shuffled in and out of the arcade moving pinballs, a riding horse, candy machines, and other amusements out into the adjacent parking lot. Laparco was still barefoot, Willis wore pants and shoes but no shirt, and Steve was fully dressed, hair slicked back neatly. His white shirt was smeared with soot and grime.

Mel parked the truck and ran straight to Al Johnson. The chief was suited up in full gear and directing his two hose teams when Mel grabbed him by the shoulder. Before he could speak, Johnson said, "It's pretty bad, Mel. Don't get any closer." The intense heat stung Mel's face from a hundred feet away. Both fire trucks were at the site now but only one was pumping. The second crew scrambled to get into the fight.

Mel heard an unrecognizable voice behind him.

"Sorry, Mel, we'll do our best to save her," the man said, disappearing into the haze before he could see his face. He headed over toward Steve, Willis, and Laparco. Rita stood under a tree on the edge of the lot where the vending machines sat. Without saying a word, Mel joined in and the four men quickly removed the last three machines from the arcade.

Willis and Laparco gasped for air and collapsed to the ground, leaning against the tree where Rita stood. Steve walked over to join them and calmly lit a cigarette.

"Not much we can do now, my friend," Steve said to Mel. Rita was at Mel's side as the five of them stood back, watching the tragedy unfold. By now, every available volunteer was at the site. Fuzzy hangovers were erased by adrenaline and determination. Most of the men fighting the fire had grown up at the Beach and remembered eating at the Shack as kids, long before Mel Rosco took it over.

A large group of spectators had assembled at the scene. Among them were Jimmy and Diane Rosco, who sat in their car, apart from the crowd.

Chief Johnson contemplated sending a man onto the roof to shoot water more effectively, but decided against it. In his heart he knew it was a lost cause. The old wooden building was destined for destruction. After twenty-six years of firefighting, he could usually tell within fifteen minutes how long it would take to extinguish the flames. This building was over fifty years old, poorly constructed of pine, and coated with layer upon layer of oil paint. Inside it was chock-full of flammables — paper products, towels, rags, and a dozen five gallon tins of peanut oil Mel had ordered for the season.

At 4:30 a.m. Chief Johnson spotted a visible shift in the building as it canted to one side. He gave the order for his men to retreat. Slowly, the hose crews eased back twenty paces, all the time pouring water onto the endless inferno.

A fireman shouted, "There she goes!" In what appeared to be slow motion, the structure creaked loudly, leaned at a thirty-degree angle, and then collapsed in on itself. A burst of sparks and debris flew in all directions. The crowd instinctively shielded their faces and backed away. What had been a family's way of life a few hours ago was now a smoldering pile of rubble. Only one wall was left standing erect, like a punched-out prize fighter refusing to go down. Mel held Rita close to him. Tears flowed from his wife's eyes and her body shook uncontrollably. Steve and his boys remained at their side.

Once the building crumbled, it took only minutes for the hose teams to extinguish the blaze. The steady breeze that had fanned the flames died down. Smoke and heat began to rise straight up rather than blowing sideways and the air cleared.

It was nearly 6 a.m. when Chief Johnson approached Mel and Rita, who now sat on folding beach chairs that a good Samaritan had provided them.

"Mel, when you're ready, we need to talk about how this happened," the chief said.

Mel took a deep breath, never taking his eyes off the rubble. After a few seconds he turned toward Johnson and said, "Al, it was such an old building I guess it could have been anything. We doubled checked that all the equipment was off before locking up. That's the only thing I can think of now."

"The state inspectors will be here sometime this morning and they'll want to see your documents," said the chief.

"Yeah, I know. Rita's got those on file somewhere," replied Mel.

"Yes, I do," she said.

"I know it's awfully early to hit you two with this kind of stuff, but with the amount of resources we expended tonight they'll dig pretty deep into the investigation. Do you have insurance?"

As soon as the words came out of Al Johnson's mouth he wished he could have taken them back.

"Sure Al, we have a mortgage, and the bank requires that," Mel answered directly. He was irritated that Al had asked the question.

"Oh, that's right, of course you would," Chief Johnson said, moving on to another subject. "It'll take an hour or so for us to wrap up here. Can I do anything for you?"

"No, no thanks," Mel and Rita both said.

The firemen had removed their heavy garb to cool off and were slowly stowing equipment and rewinding hoses. Chief Johnson ordered two men to surround the site with a temporary fence to preserve evidence until the investigators arrived. A single state trooper had come to the scene shortly after the first fire truck. He maintained a watch over the site, not so much to prevent looting — there wasn't anything there worth stealing — but to keep gawkers from hurting themselves while peering around the mess.

Chief Johnson considered having his guys knock over the lone standing wall but decided against it. It didn't appear to be a hazard since the wind had died down and the site was secure now. His years of experience taught him not to hurry when withdrawing from a scene. Even the most insignificant artifact or piece of debris could hold the answer to what caused the disaster. Wiring, switches, and dials on appliances served as concrete evidence.

Although he could not imagine the Roscos doing it, there was always the possibility of arson. Most of the village knew that

Mel was hurting financially and even the bravest of men were known to commit crimes when desperate.

Rita glanced down Park Avenue and saw Sylvia, Donny, and Dickie walking slowly toward them. Sylvia stood in the middle, one arm linked with Donny's and holding tightly to Dickie's hand. Rita stood up as the three kids descended on her in a simultaneous, crushing hug. They all began to cry as Mel watched, still seated. He forced himself to hold his head up a little higher, and held back his tears before joining them.

"Hey guys, not the best way to start Sunday morning, huh?" he said, struggling to keep from crying himself. He knew that it was his place to reassure the family that all would be OK. Breaking down now would only make matters worse.

"I guess we can miss church today," Rita added with a forced smile. She kissed her daughter lightly on the top of her head. The last of the fire crews drifted away. Chief Johnson came over to the group to say goodbye and Mel thanked him for his help. Steve, Willis, and Laparco went back to the Lakeshore to begin their daily routines. The state trooper stayed on site but was taking care of other business over his radio.

When the fire scene cleared, it was another quiet Sunday morning at the lake. The waters were dotted with fishermen castings their lines. A speed boat blazed by with a skier in tow, taking advantage of the lake's early morning smoothness.

Mel, Rita, and their children were together and safe. As they embraced on that street corner, Mel turned his thoughts toward where fate might take him after all of this, but he really didn't care. The four most important people in his life were right there by his side and, with the good Lord's help, he'd figure something out.

Rita drove the kids back home in the truck but Mel chose to stay for the time being. He knew there was nothing he could do at this point, but nonetheless felt it was his place to be there. The longer he stared at the smoldering mess, the harder it was for him to believe this was happening. Searching for something else to engage his thoughts, Mel approached the trooper's car to introduce himself. The officer had his head down and was filling out an official looking form on a clipboard. Next to him on the seat was a book of crossword puzzles. Mel knew most of the local troopers by name, but not this one. He knocked lightly on the cruiser's door and spoke first as the man looked up.

"Officer, Mel Rosco," he said, extending his hand through the open window.

The officer looked up, smiled, and said, "Tim Dirks, pleasure to meet you, sir. Is this your property?"

"Yes, what's left of it," answered Mel.

"Sorry," Dirks said.

"I haven't seen you around the Beach. Are you new?"

"Yes sir, just graduated from the Academy in May. The junior people get the weekend duty so here I am," Dirks said, hoping he hadn't brought some levity into the conversation inappropriately.

Mel didn't seem to mind and continued with the small talk. "Any family?" he asked.

"One three-year-old son. My wife and I are trying for a second."

"Well, it sure is fun trying, isn't it?" joked Mel. They both chuckled as Dirks felt more at ease talking. Mel Rosco had a gift of making strangers feel comfortable even under the worst circumstances. What he lacked in hard driving business sense, he made up for in being able to read people and understand their spirit. When you were around Mel, the world just seemed right.

"Chief Johnson tells me that your place was a real landmark here at the Beach," Dirks said.

"Yeah, it was. I took it over in '57. The old place fed a lot of people over the years. The food business is a tough one, though. That's why I started expanding into vending machines. I think there's a bright future in the coin operated amusement field. Steady cash flow and not as many headaches with inventory and health regulations. The only product that you have to provide the customer is a few laughs."

Dirks smiled and nodded in response. "Well sir, I hope everything works out for you and your family. This all must be pretty devastating," he said, trying his best to remain professional but caring at the same time.

"We'll survive. Thanks for your concern, officer." Mel patted Dirks on the shoulder as a father might when reassuring his son that he did OK.

"Any idea when the investigators might show?" Mel asked.

"The last call I got from headquarters, they said 10 a.m. They also mentioned that a BCI agent would be here as well," Dirks replied, referring to the Bureau of Criminal Investigation, a division of the New York State Police.

It wasn't unusual for a BCI agent to be sent out as part of a fire investigation. About twenty years prior, there had been a series of suspicious fires at the Beach. The BCI finally apprehended a local teenager who had started the fires out of boredom. The thrill turned into an obsession as the young arsonist ultimately destroyed two businesses and four unoccupied cottages. It took the investigators three years to put together a solid case that lead to a conviction.

"Mel?" A familiar voice called out from behind. Mel turned away from the patrol car to see Carl, Ron, and Ollie. It looked as if they had been up all night partying and just heard the news.

"Man, *what the hell happened?*" asked Ron.

"No idea, Ron," answered Mel. "I heard the siren and got a call from Steve a few minutes after that. From that point on, it's all been a blur for Rita and me." The guys stood silent, starring in disbelief. A few hours ago they'd felt like they were on top of the world. Now, their boss's business was gone and they were unemployed.

A large black sedan pulled up. It was Father Lenny, the parish priest who was on a break between the eight and ten o'clock masses. Bad news always seemed to find its way quickly to Father Lenny and the fire was no exception. Still clad in his altar vestments, he said a prayer out loud and offered his blessing to Mel and all those who had risked their lives trying to save the Shack. Mel thanked Father Lenny for coming as the priest got into his car and drove off to say his next mass.

Shortly after that, another car arrived and out stepped Moe LaGriggio, who ran a greasy spoon breakfast spot on Main Street. He carried a large tray of coffee, donuts, and raisin toast. Mel thanked him and encouraged all present to help themselves.

Mel sat back down in the lawn chair. The adrenaline that had boosted him through the night and early morning was wearing thin. He fought back the fear and anxiety that now crept over him and continued to welcome the growing crowd of well-wishers.

Chapter Seventeen

The fire investigation team arrived shortly after 10 a.m. and began sifting through the rubble for clues. They used the same checklist that the state had employed for decades, searching for signs of faulty wiring, leaking propane lines, and shorted circuits. They also scoured the site for evidence of arson: gas cans left behind, broken door hinges, and other signs of forced entry.

"What do you think, fellas?" asked Jack Barretti of the BCI. He arrived at the scene in an unmarked trooper car painted in the usual nondescript brown color that speeders and drag racers could spot a mile away. Jack had earned the privilege of driving a company car three years ago, but after twenty-two years on the force, numerous citations and decorations, his most valued accomplishment was the respect he earned from his fellow officers. He was a cop's cop. Wounded in the line of duty twice, he had the reputation of being a fearless law man with the determination of a pit bull. What he'd lost physically due to age he more than made up for with street smarts and experience.

Walking around the perimeter, Jack surveyed the site, unconsciously tugging at his shirt collar. His large neck never took to the starched white shirts and ties he now wore as a plain-clothes man. *Give me a trooper-gray outfit any day instead,* he thought. Uniforms were more comfortable and he didn't waste time every morning making a decision about what to wear.

"Oh, hi Jack," said Bill Peck, one of the inspectors. "This one's going to be tough. The old place wouldn't come close to passing the new framing codes and the wiring was inadequate even before Rosco took it over. So far though, no signs of foul play."

"Nope," added Pete Nash, the other investigator. "Pretty clean so far."

"All right, you guys, have fun. I'll be interviewing witnesses next door."

Jack stepped gingerly over the debris and headed toward the Lakeshore. When he inadvertently put his foot down on a charred bag of potatoes, his size thirteen wing tip punched through the shredded burlap, sinking ankle deep in the still-warm spuds.

"Whoa, didn't see that coming," he said.

Pete handed him a rag to clean up. As he did, he noticed a blackened twenty-five pound tin can of popping corn. Most of it had popped during the fire, blowing off the can's lid and spray-ing in all directions. The placed reeked of charred wood, burnt food, and smoke.

"Christ, what a mess!" Baretti said. Once back on the pave-ment he stomped his foot a couple times to get the last of the baked potato off his shoe.

"Mr. Rosco, sorry about your loss," said Barretti. The bar-room door closed behind him. Mel and Steve were sitting at a table having coffee. Steve had dug out an old pot from the store-room, went to the store for grinds, and brewed his own today.

"Thanks, officer," Mel replied. They'd met before, but neither felt familiar enough to be on a first name basis, especially under the circumstances.

"Mind if I join you?"

"No, please do," said Mel.

"Something to drink?" asked Steve.

"No thanks, I'm fine."

Steve and Barretti had crossed paths several times during their careers. Steve was well known around the joint circuit and the troopers were called in on a regular basis for barroom scuffles, parking lot brawls, and the less exciting cases of minors caught with bogus ID. Steve and Barretti had a mutual respect for one another despite being on opposite sides of the bar, so to speak.

"Just wanted to ask Mel a few questions," Barretti began, looking at Steve.

"Sure," said Steve. He got up and moved on to business at the other end of the barroom.

"Any idea what happened last night?" initiated Jack.

"No, nothing really comes to mind. I had a suspicion at first that one of my crew may have forgotten to turn off a deep fryer and it overheated, but my son double-checked the equipment before we closed up."

"What items are still powered when you close?" probed Barretti.

"Just the refrigerated items, ice coolers, drink machines, those things. Other than that, it's quiet and dark when we lock the door."

"Any disgruntled employees you can think of?" Jack said, looking Mel squarely in the eye. Mel was taken aback at first by the question. He couldn't imagine anyone, especially his own help, doing what the cop implied.

"Well, no, not really. We've been very lucky with our help. The young guys come and go every year but we always seem to hire familiar people — you know, someone's cousin, brother, or friend."

Over the years, Mel had in fact hired several sets of brothers or their relatives. Ollie, Ron, and Carl weren't related but had known each other since grade school. There was a family atmosphere at the Shack. The few guys who didn't finish a season usually had a legitimate reason to quit, such as finding another job, leaving the area, or just getting tired of working during summer vacation.

"OK, sir, that will do for now," Barretti stood up and extended his thick hand.

"I'll be around all day," said Mel.

"Thanks," Jack answered. He made his way across the bar to where Steve was filling a beer cooler with bottles.

"Steve, can we go into your office for a minute?"

Steve didn't reply, but finished what he was doing and walked out from behind the bar. They found a place to sit, Steve at his small desk and Jack on a chair he'd dragged in from the other room.

"Chief Johnson tells me that when he got to the firehouse last night the first person he saw was one of your hired men."

"Yeah, Anthony Laparco," Steve said. He pulled a cigarette from his second pack of the day and lit up. "He's here now if you want to talk with him."

"Sure, in good time, but there's a couple of items I want to clear up first. Johnson said Laparco was acting a little strange when he found him and wasn't wearing any shoes." Steve sat expressionless as Barretti spoke. "Where's this guy from?"

Steve took a stiff drag, blew the smoke to one side and answered. "Johnnie arranged to get him on a work program from the State School. He's hired guys from the School before to work at some of his other businesses. Laparco started here last summer."

"How's he doing?"

"Hard-working kid," Steve said, nodding his head lightly. "Willis Shank, my other guy, took him under his wing and seems pretty happy with him too. Anything else?"

"No, not now," Barretti said. "I'd like to meet Laparco, though, and Willis after that."

"OK, let me get him for you," Steve said. He butted out his smoke and left the room.

"Officer Barretti, this is Anthony Laparco," Steve said. He rested his right hand on Laparco's shoulder.

"Hello, Anthony, can we talk for a minute?" Barretti asked.

"Sure," said Laparco. Other than his embarrassing experience attempting to get a bicycle license at the troopers barracks, he'd never been this close to a cop before.

Steve left the two men alone as Barretti sat down and motioned for Laparco to do the same. The BCI man explained how he was investigating the fire and that he'd already talked to Chief Johnson. As he spoke, it was obvious that Laparco was uneasy and didn't want to be there.

"That was the right thing for you to do last night, pulling the alarm. You must have been in a real hurry. Chief Johnson said you forgot to put on your shoes," Barretti said. He smiled a bit, hoping to put Laparco at ease.

"Actually they were my shower shoes and I couldn't run very fast with them on, so I kicked them off." He went on to describe how he couldn't sleep and had gone for a short walk around the backside of Mel Rosco's business. That's when he saw the smoke and flames in the upstairs windows.

Jack listened intently, all the while observing the young man's mannerisms. This was his first time interviewing a former mental patient and he was doing his best not to allow that fact to taint his judgment, but his instincts told him something wasn't right here. The guy seemed nervous and fidgety. A light coat of perspiration sprung up from Laparco's brow. This wasn't unusual for someone being questioned, but what caught Barretti's attention was that the more Laparco talked, the more agitated he seemed. Normally, it worked the other way; an innocent person became more relaxed as the interrogation progressed.

Barretti could not have known that the mention of the shower shoes had triggered deep memories for Anthony Laparco. They had been issued to him four years ago at the State School. Laparco understood the questions and responded, but a part of his brain had detached and returned to the sights, sounds, and smells of the institution he never wanted to see again.

Despite his quirkiness and bizarre looks, Laparco did not belong with the mental patients at the School. Sadly, he joined a sizable group of poor souls put there for one simple reason: nobody cared. With nowhere else to go, the State School became his home. The physical and mental abuse he witnessed there bored deeper into his consciousness than those who were mentally afflicted and didn't know right from wrong. He'd been punished and harassed by big, official looking men — men not unlike Jack Barretti in appearance.

Will the State School somehow find out about this and make me go back? Laparco wondered. As he sat across from Barretti he became terrified: in his mind, he was the prey and Jack Barretti was the hunter.

"Did you see anyone else or anything suspicious while you were walking around Mr. Rosco's property?" Barretti asked.

Laparco did his best to stay calm but failed miserably. "What, what do you mean?" he stammered.

"You know, someone out for a walk, passing cars, that sort of thing." He smiled and gestured good naturedly with his hands, trying again to help Laparco relax, but fear shot out from the young man's eyes. The BCI agent had learned early in his career that reliable facts seldom came from a frightened witness.

Laparco's mind jumped to the bike rider who had bolted past him just short of the firehouse. Neglecting that fact, instead he answered, "Well, I did see a car coming from the other direction when I was running down Main Street, but it turned down a side street before I could see what kind it was or who was driving."

The room grew silent. Barretti's instincts signaled there was something more to the story but decided to let it go for the time being. The smile left his face. "Anything else you would like to add, Anthony?" Jack said, gathering his notes.

"No sir, that's about it."

"OK, thanks for your time and have a good day," He snapped his briefcase shut and headed for the door.

"OK, you too," Laparco replied as he followed Barretti out of Steve's office. Last night while running down Main Street, it had been dark and he had been panicky. He didn't remember many details along the way. He never got a good look at the rider's face but he had recognized the flashy banana seat bike in an instant. It belonged to Freddy Rosco.

Chapter Eighteen

Business went on as usual that holiday weekend at the Beach. Tourists lingered and gawked as they passed the Shack's burned-out hulk on their way to the water. The fire had been extinguished for hours, but the prevailing westerly breeze carried the burnt, smoky smell throughout the midway. Officer Dirks put up a more secure fence and several "No Trespassing" signs around the scene. Willis and Laparco returned and helped Mel move the vending machines back into the arcade. The small building was scorched outside, but intact, and suitable to store the machines. The door that Steve had wisely ordered knocked down was barricaded with plywood, and Willis had rechecked the security of the other doors and windows. Although unlikely, there was always a chance of vandalism and looting. Realizing there really wasn't anything else for them to do, Mel thanked the two men and they walked back to work at the Lakeshore.

Pete Nash and Bill Peck started wrapping up their investigation around 3:30 p.m. The midday heat had set in and both men were battling dehydration. The stench of burnt lumber and food was imbedded in their noses and all they wanted to do was go home, shower, and be with their families. For them, the Sunday of this July Fourth weekend was turning into just another workday.

Mel Rosco approached them as they loaded the last of their tools and notebooks into the truck.

"Mr. Rosco, we normally avoid contact with the property owners during an investigation," said Pete.

"Sure, I can appreciate that," Mel said.

"Well, I'm going to break with procedure for a minute and tell you how badly we both feel for you. The Beach lost a landmark and you lost your business."

"Thanks, my family and I appreciate that, really," replied Mel. Pete and Bill climbed into their truck as Mel stood to the side.

"Oh, here," said Bill, reaching into a tattered canvas bag between his legs. "Figured this must belong to one of your kids. It's pretty dirty and needs a new lens cover but you might be able to get it working again."

Mel couldn't make out what the metal object was at first, but once in his hand he realized it was a flashlight. Starring down at it, he didn't know what to say other than "thanks."

"Take care now," Pete said, waving his hand out the window as the two men drove away. Mel didn't reply but simply waved back. He glanced down again at the flashlight. He recognized the Boy Scout emblem embossed on its side. Engraved just to the right of the emblem was the name, ROSCO. Neither Donny nor Dickie had ever been Scouts. He tucked the flashlight away in his pocket and started walking home.

When he arrived there, Mel found Rita and Laparco sitting at the kitchen table. Rita had laid out a plate of cookies for her guest. Laparco ate four of them and was working on his second glass of milk.

"Hey, what's up?" Mel asked.

"Hi, Mel," Laparco said as he stood up.

"I've got some laundry to fold upstairs," Rita said. She sensed it was time to excuse herself and leave the two men alone. When he'd come into the house, all that Laparco had told her was, "I have to talk to Mel." She could tell by his mannerisms how nervous he was. The cookies and milk had calmed him down a bit and they were just starting to chat when Mel came in.

"Mel, I've got something to say to you in private," Laparco said. His eyes followed Rita as she climbed the stairs.

"How about we take a drive, then?" Mel suggested.

"Yeah, right," Laparco said. He was already out the door before Mel reached for his truck keys.

They were both silent as Mel drove a couple miles away from town. Unable to contain himself any longer, Laparco finally blurted out, "Mel, last night when I was running to the firehouse, I think I saw your nephew riding his bike."

Mel had to think twice whom Laparco was talking about. The families were so distant he didn't correlate Freddy as his nephew at first.

"What?" said Mel.

"Just before I turned into the firehouse driveway, a bike cut right in front of me. I didn't see his face but I knew it was Freddy's bike and it looked like him from behind."

Mel thought to himself, *Yup, Freddy is pretty distinguishable, especially from the rear.*

Freddy prided himself in the fact that nobody at the Beach had a bicycle like his — big, flashy, and painted bright orange. *As usual, nothing but the best for Jimmy's kid,* Mel thought. Laparco could only dream of having such a nice bike. The one that he and Willis had salvaged from the dump had a bent frame, different sized tires, and pink pedals pulled off another junker. To him, Freddy's sleek ride looked like a Cadillac.

"When the cop talked to me today, I didn't say anything about it, Freddy being your family and all. I thought I should tell you first," Laparco said.

Mel sat quietly for a moment and then said, "Anthony, you shouldn't lie to the cops. This is serious business."

"But I didn't lie, Mel. He asked me if I saw anybody else taking a walk or any cars around your place and I said the truth, that was 'no.' Then he asked me if there was anything else that I *wanted* to add and I said 'no' because there wasn't. I was a little scared talking to him because he looked at me funny, like I did it. Mel, do you think Freddy had something to do with the fire?"

Mel was surprised by Laparco's intuitiveness. The fellow's appearance led people to think he was a half-wit, but having known him for a couple years Mel knew otherwise. Beyond his comical looks and emotional problems the man had some smarts.

"I don't know, Anthony. Maybe it's best if we just keep this between you and me for a while. Thanks for letting me know."

They drove back to Mel's place. Laparco hopped out, got on his bicycle, and rode away. Mel sat in the truck for a while thinking about the words he'd just heard. He pulled the small flashlight from his pocket and hid it behind some papers in the truck's glove compartment.

"What did Laparco want?" asked Rita when Mel walked back into the house.

"Not much. He was just a little scared talking to the trooper and I tried to reassure him that things would be OK. He might think someone suspects that he set the fire."

"What do you think, could he have done it?"

"Honey, that kid doesn't have a mean bone in his body. I suppose anything is possible, but my gut tells me he wouldn't do something like that. Geez, Rita, he's practically family."

Mel sat down at the kitchen table with his wife. The boys were out doing something and John had called Sylvia for a date, so it was just the two of them at home.

"When is the last time I was home on a Sunday night in July?" asked Mel.

"God, so long that I can't remember," Rita said with a laugh.

"Hey, how about we go see a movie tonight?"

"Are you serious?" she asked.

"Come on, let's go!" Mel replied.

With that, Rita wrote a quick note to the kids telling them where they were. The two of them got into Rita's station wagon and drove off. It had been years since they last went on a date. They traveled to a drive-in theater and watched a corny Western, talking and joking through the whole thing. For a few short hours they were free from the worry and angst of what the future might hold for them. On the way home, they stopped for ice cream.

Chapter Nineteen

Monday, July Fourth arrived right on time. Today was the icing on the cake for the rest of the Beach merchants. This weekend was shaping up to truly be golden: everyone was doing record sales. The weather was perfect and, with fireworks scheduled at 10 p.m., there would be a full day of celebration and spending by the tourists. The crowd never left before the fireworks. Amusement rides, restaurants, novelty shops, and joints would all be open by noon in anticipation of a solid ten to twelve hours of business.

People were lined up for breakfast at Jimmy's Shoreline Inn by nine o'clock. That rarely happened. Moe LaGriggio normally handled most of the early morning diners, but his place was packed by 7:30 and the overflow migrated down the street to Jimmy's.

Rita and the kids converged in their kitchen, all wearing a "what do we do now?" look on their faces. The events of Sunday morning had left them all a little shell-shocked. Now, after a decent night's sleep, they were rested but unsure of how to spend the day.

Donny broke the silence and asked, "Dad, I was wondering if the family had any plans for the day?"

"Well, son, not really. How about you, Mom?" Mel said, turning to his wife.

"You know, we've never had a July Fourth off, so maybe we should do something different. How about a picnic?"

Everyone agreed with Rita and sprung into to action, preparing food to take and loading the car with folding chairs, blankets, and what not. They headed out on the thirty-minute drive to one of the area's favorite state parks, Chittenango Falls. No one could remember the last time the family had done something like this. The ride to the park started out with everyone joking and talking about how nice it was to be together today and not be working. After ten minutes of that, however, the stark reality set in of what had happened. The rest of the drive they sat quietly and just enjoyed the scenery.

At some point during the ride, every one of them contemplated what might lie ahead for the family. At one end of the spectrum, Mel wondered how he was going earn a living and support his family. At the other end, young Dickie worried about where he could find a job to make some money and expand his model car collection.

Once at the Falls, happiness returned and the Roscos did what any other family would do on such a day — they had fun. It was a beautiful afternoon. They tossed a football that Donny had brought along, swung on the swing set, and walked down to the bottom of the Falls. Standing there before the roaring water, Donny wondered aloud how cold the water was. Without hesitation Mel said, "Let's find out." He grabbed his unsuspecting son by the arm, yanking him into the stream and under the cascading water. They both yipped with exhilaration. The water was cold! As they jumped back onto the banks of the stream, Rita,

Sylvia, and Dickie were howling with laughter. Mel and Donny caught their breath and joined in. Their soaked sneakers made squishing sounds as they hiked back up the trail to their car. Mel wasn't sure what caused him to pull such a stunt, but welcomed the comic relief it brought everyone.

On the drive home, Mel said, "That was fun. We should do stuff like this more often. Sylvia and Dickie, it's your turn under the falls next time!" This launched the group into more banter and teasing about the day's events. No one wanted it to end. Their conversation faded, however, as they drove over the canal bridge and the sight of the bustling amusement park unfolded before them. The black scar that was once the Shack stood out as the only spot in the park that wasn't teeming with people and activity. Rita looked at her husband and saw the sorrow in his eyes that only she could detect. So far today, Mel had put on a good face for the kids, but he couldn't fool his wife. She knew that he was coming to grips with the fact that their lives would never be the same again. The Shack was gone and with it the very heart of their world at Woodland Beach. Rita felt a chill down her spine at the thought of what changes might lie ahead for her family.

The Roscos spent the rest of the day doing what everyone else did — enjoying time off and waiting for the fireworks. The family agreed that the best place to watch the display would be on the shore by the amusement park. At 9:30, they joined the throng migrating in that direction. Several friends sought out Mel during the walk and continued to greet the family as they stood in the sand waiting for the show to begin. The anticipation finally ended as the calm night sky erupted with burst of colors and bone-rattling thuds. The display would continue for nearly thirty minutes, each rocket streaking upward and transforming nighttime into a slice of daylight.

Donny turned his sight away from the fireworks to observe the faces of people around him. The illumination of every round created a different picture. Some people were smiling, some were expressionless. Others stood motionless with their mouths open in awe. Little children, many witnessing the display for the first time, squealed with pleasure. Between salvos came the sounds of happiness and revelry that rise from a crowd having a good time.

As the celebration reached its grand finale, Donny looked over at his parents. He saw his father standing behind his mother, arms draped over her shoulders in a gentle hug. It was at that moment Donny knew that his family would get through this. The financial setbacks, burdens, and worries could not topple their spirit. Donny realized that his dad wasn't motivated by greed, anger, or envy. Mel loved his family. He knew who and what he was, and stayed within himself. Suddenly, it occurred to Donny why so many people loved his father: Mel Rosco was the real deal.

When the show ended, the Roscos drifted with the crowd returning to their cars and homes. The last two days had worn them down and they were exhausted. All of them, from Mel to little Dickie, knew that change was in the wind, but no one could imagine the direction events were about to take. Donny Rosco would never forget this day, July Fourth, 1966.

Chapter Twenty

The phone rang; it was the insurance agent handling the claim for the Shack. He relayed a message that the inspectors had found some suspicious evidence by the deep fryers and wanted to see Mel at the site as soon as possible. Rita left for work at the post office. She looked forward to getting out of the house and thinking about something other than her family's problems. Mel drove by himself to meet the insurance man and fire investigators at the Shack.

"Hi, Mel," said Phil Graff. He ran a small branch office in town and took care of insurance needs for most of the beach merchants.

"Never dreamed that anything like this could ever happen," said Mel, shaking his head.

"Most people don't. That's why I'm in business. Come on over here, will ya?" Phil said. He walked slowly through the debris to the spot where the remains of the four deep fryers stood.

"Bill found what might be the source of the fire near the big fryer." Phil pointed to the charred remains of the blancher, which precooked the French fries.

"The fire clearly started here," Bill said. "You see the way this charred wood looks different than the surrounding area? We call that 'gatoring.' That, coupled with the 'V' patterning of the burn above the fryers, is our evidence. If one of these fryers were left on during the night or malfunctioned internally, it could have caused an overheated condition. The oil level would have lowered as it smoldered, exposing the electric heating element. Any burnt bits of potato or other residue in the oil would have lowered the flash point as well. Once flames ignited on the oil surface, the stainless steel on the wall and exhaust hood would help contain the fire for a while, but not for that long. I imagine, by the nature of your business, you had a large number of flammables such as paper goods nearby."

Mel nodded and listened intently as Bill continued. "Any build-up of grease on the vent fan and ducting above the fire would have ignited and carried intense heat to the second floor making the situation even worse."

Phil Graff took Mel aside asked privately, "When was the last time the exhaust fan and chimney were cleaned?"

"I replaced the fan two years ago," said Mel. "The duct work hasn't been touched since I bought the place." His face reddened with embarrassment.

"Well, don't feel too badly," said Phil. "I'd wager that many of the Beach establishments are in the same boat. And quite frankly, the county and state inspectors don't always do their best to ensure a thorough inspection. I have copies of your inspections for the last five years and you're current. I can't see any hang-ups here, Mel. When these guys are ready to make a decision, my company is prepared to move ahead with granting your claim so you can start rebuilding."

Mel was surprised at how quickly the whole process was coming to a conclusion. He didn't understand all the technical talk, but knew enough about cooking to realize how oil could be heated to the point of combustion. Mel and Phil rejoined the investigators, who were talking amongst themselves. Bill handed a clipboard over to Pete, who assumed the role of spokesman.

"We've found no evidence of foul play. Our report will state that we attribute the fire to an unexplained malfunction of one of your deep fryers. The large gap of time that elapsed — we estimate one to two hours — between the fire's start and it being detected allowed it to smolder, flare up, and then spread at a rapid pace. The fire department had little if any chance of saving the structure and its contents. The age of the building, method of construction, and high volume of flammables inside further aggravated the situation."

Mel took it all in, weighing every word spoken. He felt that the three men standing before him had done their damnedest to complete the job honestly, efficiently, and in the best interests of the community. He also sensed that no one wanted to drag this out. He wasn't surprised when Bill Peck spoke up.

"Mel, off the record, everyone here knows what a setback this is for you. We wish you, Rita, and the kids all the best and hope you bounce back real soon." Bill paused, looked Mel straight in the eye and shook his hand. "Hurry up and rebuild, OK? I miss those tasty fries already!"

Mel laughed politely at Bill's sincere attempt to lighten the mood. The four men started walking to their vehicles. Mel thanked them as Bill and Pete got into their truck and drove off. He stood silently next to Phil Graff for a few seconds before speaking.

"Phil, Rita and I only carried enough insurance on the place to keep the bank happy. We've leveraged ourselves pretty deep over the years. I don't think there will be near enough money to rebuild, considering today's material costs and tighter building codes. Besides, most of my cooking equipment is still being paid off as well. This place is our main source of income, and with the rest of the summer shot, I'm not sure what the hell we're going to do."

"I know, Mel," said Phil. He'd been in the insurance business for thirty-five years and knew how a fire could devastate. When it wiped out a man's livelihood it was even more tragic. Mel and Rita had little equity in their home and couldn't count on that to help. Phil was also Jimmy Rosco's agent. He didn't care to know the details of the divide that existed between the two men, but nonetheless, he also couldn't imagine someone refusing to help a blood relative in need. Maybe Jimmy would come to the aid of his brother, Phil thought.

"I've got to get back to the office," Phil said, looking down at his watch.

"See you later, Phil, thanks again." They shook hands through Phil's car window. As he drove away, Mel stood alone on the sidewalk and turned toward the Shack. He gazed at the ruins, focusing on the one wall still standing. Chief Johnson had told him that, for safety reasons, it would have to be knocked down once the investigation was complete. Located at the top of the wall were two windows underneath what used to be small gables on the second floor. There was something about those windows that caught Mel's eye. The sheer force of the flames had busted out the glass and the white painted frames were fused to a black char. As he walked closer, Mel now saw what had triggered his curiosity. Chief Johnson had missed it, and so had the two fire investigators and the insurance agent. One of the window sashes was wide open.

Chapter Twenty-one

Freddy Rosco gradually came out of his funk. He poured himself a huge bowl of chocolate flavored cereal and joined his parents at the breakfast table. The two of them were discussing how tired the Shoreline's staff was after the busy holiday weekend. Jimmy had cut back on his workers for the remainder of the week, asking for volunteers. Four of his wait staff and two cooks gratefully took his offer for some needed rest.

"Jimmy, we netted over four thousand dollars this weekend," Diane said. She was seated at a small desk where Jimmy kept his accounting records at their house. Although Diane had nothing to do with running the business, she did pay close attention to how much money was coming in. "What do you think about giving everyone a twenty dollar bonus when you do payroll this week?"

Jimmy sat patiently and heard out his wife, pretending to weigh her suggestion. He wanted Diane to think that he valued her opinion, although actually, he couldn't care less.

"Well, the only thing wrong with that is some of them might think they deserve a bonus every time they work hard. With the hourly rate we pay plus the big tip revenues this weekend, they all did well enough. Besides, nobody ever did me favors like that."

"But it would only cost us a few hundred dollars and. . ." Freddy was surprised to hear a hint of compassion in his mother's voice.

"Nope," Jimmy said, interrupting her while he put his plate and coffee cup in the sink. With the issue closed, he picked up his clipboard and went to work.

Diane sat stymied as Jimmy walked out. Freddy stared straight ahead and continued shoveling down his cereal.

"Good morning, Jimmy. You had a couple of calls," said Tony, the Shoreline's day manager. He'd been the restaurant's open-up guy for six years and Jimmy considered him the best of his three managers.

"Who was it?" Jimmy asked.

"He wouldn't say, but it sounded like your brother Mel. He called twice and each time he said he'd call back later."

"OK, thanks." Jimmy said. He sat down at the desk he kept on site at the Shoreline. Jimmy had taken over a small storeroom as his auxiliary office. As he fine-tuned the operation over the years, he found he needed this place to sit down, make phone calls, and plan work schedules. The area served as an oasis when he wanted a break. Ten minutes into his routine of going over invoices and messages, the phone rang.

"We need to talk," said the voice on the other end. It was Mel. Jimmy hadn't said a word to his brother since the fire. Diane had put aside her anger at Rita and urged him to call but Jimmy refused, rationalizing that "Mel had enough on his plate right now" and he'd call later.

"Sorry about the fire, Mel. I'm glad no one was hurt."

Mel didn't engage in conversation, but stated bluntly, "I'll meet you at the stone barn in thirty minutes." It was more of an order than a request. Jimmy sensed the indignation in his brother's voice, but wasn't sure what this was about. *If Mel wants to ask me for money, this sure isn't the way to do it*, he thought.

"I gotta make a few calls first. How about an hour from now?" he offered.

"All right, an hour then," Mel said and hung up the phone.

The two men were headed to a spot about a mile inland from the lake's northeast shore. During the twenty-minute ride, Jimmy searched his brain for what this could be about. Mel sounded pissed off. He decided to proceed cautiously: growing up, Jimmy had learned that he could only push his good-natured brother so far before he would strike back. Jimmy was physically superior and had won most of their childhood fights. He understood, however, his brother's inexhaustible determination and pride. He secretly admired this trait in Mel because deep in his soul he knew he possessed neither of these qualities. Oh, he put up a good front when people were watching, and he had convinced the town he was worthy of the position he held in the community. In his heart of hearts, though, he knew that neither he nor Diane could endure the life that Mel and Rita had. And how on earth did they raise such great kids? His Freddy was a spoiled, deplorable child in everyone's eyes. Few people had the guts to point this out to him or Diane, but they both knew it. Rosa had given up years ago trying to mend the fences between Jimmy and his brother. After the fire, neither Jimmy nor Mel called Pennsylvania to tell her the news. *What difference could she make anyway?* they thought.

Apprehension crept over him as he turned off the main highway onto a gravel road. Not knowing what this meeting was about, he felt totally unprepared. Jimmy hated that feeling. His fears subsided when he saw his brother at the end of road. Mel had already parked by the barn and was leaning against his truck with arms crossed.

The meeting place was an abandoned farm known for its big barn constructed of stone. It had been built by German immigrants at the turn of the century and for over thirty years served as a working dairy farm. Vandals had set the barn ablaze in 1941, destroying it, as the stone walls offered little protection to its wooden interior and roof. The fire burned uncontrollably, fueled by bales of hay packed into the barn's loft in preparation for winter. The raging inferno could be seen from the other side of the lake, over ten miles away. All but a few of the dairy cows and farm animals inside were lost.

The Germans were so devastated that they abandoned the place shortly thereafter and left the area. Folklore spread over the years that a group of Nazi haters were responsible for the tragedy and had taken out their anger on the peaceful farmers. No one was ever charged with the crime. Since then, the place had continued to deteriorate; the last two decades, it became a favorite hangout for under-age drinking parties. Beer bottles, fire pits, and junk littered the grounds.

When Mel drove up to the barn, he was struck by the irony of choosing a burned-out building as their meeting place. The fact hadn't crossed his mind when he'd called Jimmy.

"What's up, Mel?" Jimmy asked as he got out of his car.

Mel disregarded the pleasantries and got right to his point. "I have reason to believe that your son knows something about my fire," he said.

"Like what?" Jimmy asked. The outrageous claim nearly caused him to laugh, but he checked himself. He failed, however, to mask the smugness covering his face.

Mel hated this arrogant side of his brother. He'd spent his childhood as the recipient of his Jimmy's barbs and things hadn't changed much since then. Without saying a word Jimmy's eyes demanded, "Prove it."

"Anthony Laparco saw somebody riding their bicycle across Main Street when he ran to pull the alarm Saturday night. He didn't see the rider's face but he recognized the bike and it looked like Freddy from behind."

Jimmy had the same thought as Mel when visualizing Freddy riding the fancy bike. The kid was imposing and hard to miss even in the faint illumination of the streetlights.

"Are you kidding? With that you think you solved the case and you're ready to hang it on my son?" Jimmy regretted the words as soon as they left his mouth. Seeing this had torqued Mel, he backed off and mellowed his tone. "Well, what do you think he knows?"

"I'm not sure, but it just doesn't set well with me. I haven't gone to the cops yet, but you better get some answers from Freddy,"

Jimmy knew his brother was dead serious. His mind flashed ahead to what it would mean if Mel was onto something and Freddy actually knew who'd set the fire or, worse yet, had done it himself.

"Does anybody else know about this?"

"No," replied Mel, "just you, me, and Laparco."

Jimmy looked away and smiled. "And you're going to believe that nut?" he said, now convinced that the conversation had gotten ridiculous. "Half the town including Al Johnson thinks *he* did it. Word around the troopers' barracks is he all but confessed to Barretti."

Jimmy couldn't stomach beach rats like Laparco and Willis; he considered them low life. Once, he'd caught Willis bartering with one of his cooks and went berserk outside the Shoreline. The guy had agreed to haul some garbage to the Dumpster in return for a sandwich, but when Willis emerged from the restaurant's back door, Jimmy grabbed the food, tossed it in the dirt and then went back inside to fire the woman on the spot.

Mel walked closer to his brother and stared him in the eye. "You've got until tomorrow to talk with Freddy and get his side of the story."

"Then what?" Jimmy asked.

"Use your imagination, Jimmy, you're a smart guy." Mel didn't wait for a response. He got into his truck and left Jimmy standing there alone wondering what the hell was going on. If there was one thing Jimmy hated more than anything, it was not being in control, and right now he felt helpless.

Chapter Twenty-two

On the drive back to the Beach, Jimmy regained his composure. His thoughts shifted back to the deliberate, calculating style of reasoning for which he was known. He looked at his watch: 12:30. He still had plenty of time to sort things out.

If Mel's claim was true, Freddy's involvement with the Shack fire could be devastating to him and Diane. All his hard work, building a small fortune from nothing and gaining rank in the village, would be swept down the drain overnight. Maybe he could use his contacts to sniff and see what direction the fire investigation was taking, he thought. He knew Jack Barretti. A few years ago he and Diane had had dinner with the BCI agent and his wife when their paths crossed in Florida. That was a purely social encounter, though, and he was not sure how the man would react to hearing from him out of the blue. Right now, however, he needed to sit Freddy down and ask some questions.

Mel didn't breathe a word of his suspicions to anyone, not even Rita. She had her hands full trying to keep the family on track and maintaining some semblance of normalcy at the post office, he reasoned. Rita put on a pleasant face when friends offered their assistance, but she knew they were only being polite: there really wasn't much that could be done to help her and Mel dig out from this catastrophe. This was something that she, Mel, and the kids would have to weather alone.

The shock of the event was wearing off and the cold reality of the situation set in — a family deep in debt with its primary breadwinner out of work. They might have considered calling on Rita's family for help, but both of her parents were deceased and her brother and sister had left the area years ago. Her siblings were both holding their own financially, but were in no position to rescue them, not that she and Mel would ever allow that to happen.

Mel and Rita enjoyed their independence and knew that charity would come at a price neither of them wanted to pay. Mel always said that family, money, and business never mixed well and Rita agreed. Over the years they'd witnessed family members stop speaking when, through no fault of their own, one had been placed in a position of financial servitude to another. Good intentions were almost always lost when greed and jealousy stepped in.

Jimmy arrived back at the Shoreline and Tony assured him that all was well with the restaurant. It was a typical July Tuesday: a steady flow of customers but nothing overwhelming.

"Tony, I'll be at home until after dinner. If anyone calls, unless it's urgent, just take a message," Jimmy asked.

"Sure, Jim. Say hi to Diane for me."

Jimmy headed out the door again, feeling more relaxed with Tony at the helm and business at a lull. Upon arriving home he found an empty house. Tacked on the fridge was a note from Diane saying that she'd gone shopping. Jimmy shook his head. *How many new outfits does a woman need?* he thought. He set the note down and called out for Freddy, who wasn't there either.

Jimmy welcomed the time alone to gather his thoughts. Mel's revelation had knocked him for a loop and he was still reeling from its implications. Jimmy had next to nothing to do with his brother nowadays, and had forgotten what he was like when angry. Mel put a fear into him he hadn't felt in years.

Jimmy sat at the kitchen table and re-read Diane's note: "Gone shopping. Home around three." The note wasn't signed; there were no terms of affection like "dear" or "love.'" *It wasn't always like this*, he remembered.

Diane Draper came from a well-to-do family on Long Island and, although she spent less and less time with them as years passed, she'd never lost her taste for the finer things in life. There was always plenty of money to spend growing up on the Island. Her father, a career banker, was good with numbers and managed the family's finances like he did his business.

When she was in grade school, her father received a promotion that required commuting to the bank's corporate headquarters in New York City. At first, the family missed the free time he'd had while serving as a local branch manager less than five minutes from their home. The promotion meant that he spent over two hours each day riding on the Long Island Railroad and subway system. Add to that an eight to ten hour workday and there wasn't much time left for Diane, her mother and two sisters. The man tried his best to compensate on the weekends, but he was usually so exhausted by then that all he wanted to do was just rest or play a round of golf with his buddies. His wages nearly doubled after the promotion, though, which allowed his family to enjoy the fruits of his labors. He showered them with money and gifts, hoping to make up somehow for his absence. Diane, her mother and sisters became regulars at the high-end shops around Nassau County, spending freely on themselves as they chose. Once a month they trekked into the city for a day of shopping, lunch, and a Broadway show.

When Diane met Jimmy Rosco at the Beach, his brash, confident style swept her away. The parents of one of her girlfriends owned a cottage at Indian Lake and she spent a month vacationing there during the summer of her nineteenth year. He was twenty-three years old, and just discharged from the Navy after a two year hitch cruising the world. His handsome looks and tales of shipboard travel in the South Pacific captivated her.

Diane felt as if she'd found her Prince Charming. Sitting on the beach one night, Jimmy explained that his job as a cook was only temporary; he would have his own place someday and make a ton of money. He even showed her sketches of the restaurant layout and a menu he'd developed.

Life in the crowded suburbs was growing dull for Diane and she dreamed of leaving that for the serene beauty of life at the lake. Later that year, when Jimmy asked her to marry him, she jumped at the opportunity to make a change.

Jimmy kept his word. During the next twenty years he built the Shoreline into one of the most well known eating establishments in the area. He invested his time and money wisely achieving moderate success in other business ventures. When Freddy came along, she and Jimmy had been married eight years. Two years into Freddy's life, about the time when a second child would have been a natural desire, they agreed not to have any more children. By now, Jimmy had become a workaholic. The peaceful lakeside living that had appealed to her in the beginning grew tedious and routine. Once Freddy was in school, Diane spent little time at home during the day, preferring to shop or treat herself at the beauty parlor. Rosa looked in on Freddy when she wasn't working, but most days after school, he came home to an empty house.

The door opened and Jimmy snapped out of his daydream.

"Hi Dad," said Freddy. He was surprised to see his father home at this hour of the day.

"Where's your mother?"

"I think she was going to the beauty parlor and then shopping," Freddy answered. He wasn't really sure, but figured that was a safe guess.

It was already 2:30 and Jimmy knew he could expect her home soon. *If Diane was one thing, she was punctual*, thought Jimmy. She lived and died by her planning calendar.

"I'm going to my room to watch some TV," said Freddy. He hoped that his father would give him a good reason to do something else. Toss a football, take a bike ride, anything most dads did with their kids.

"OK," said Jimmy. Freddy lowered his head and shuffled down the hallway. Jimmy sat at the kitchen table sipping iced tea. *Should he talk about this with Diane alone or just launch into it with Freddy there too?* The door opened again, followed by the rustling of shopping bags.

"What are you doing home?" Diane said. She sounded surprised and slightly irritated. Her hands were filled with loot from a local women's store.

"I met with Mel today. There's something we need to discuss," Jimmy said. Diane set her purse and shopping bags on the counter.

"Oh really, I can only imagine. That family is in a real mess. What'd he want, money?" Despite her in-laws' tragedy, Diane was still resentful from her conversation with Rita the other day. She lit a cigarette and joined her husband at the table.

"This is serious, Diane," Jimmy said flatly.

Freddy had heard his mother come in and charged into the room. "Hi Mom!" he said. Other than this morning at breakfast, he hadn't seen his parents together all week. He welcomed the chance to spend time with them.

"Freddy, please sit down. We need to discuss something." Jimmy looked at his wife briefly and then turned directly to his son. He couldn't think of any other way to do this.

"Freddy, do you know anything about how the fire started at the Shack Saturday night?"

Diane's jaw dropped and her eyes jumped from Jimmy to her son in disbelief. Freddy's face turned red and his lower lip started to quiver. Any inner strength he might have relied on over the last few days began to evaporate. He'd spent little time thinking of how he would react if someone found out about what had happened and his young brain wasn't prepared for the rush of emotions he felt. The room fell silent as Jimmy waited for his answer. Diane, still dumbfounded, groped for something to say or do, but came up empty. She and Jimmy stared at their son. His entire body was shaking now and the color of his face darkened, becoming almost purple. Jimmy and Diane braced themselves for what they now feared was true.

Freddy tried desperately to speak, but the words wouldn't come out. Struggling to breathe, he finally stammered, "I jus, jus, just wanted to . . ." At that point, the forces of grief and shame overpowered him. His head fell to the table and he burst into uncontrolled crying.

Neither Jimmy nor Diane made any attempt to console him as they sat there confused and bewildered. After a couple minutes, Freddy's sobbing lessened and Diane spoke up. She knew this was no time for anger and if she ever needed to be a loving parent, it was now.

"What happened, Freddy?" Diane asked. She reached out and softly touched him.

For the next hour and a half, Freddy explained how a seemingly harmless prank had turned into a nightmare.

Chapter Twenty-three

After the incident with the mini bike, Freddy had begun to formulate a plot for revenge. At first he thought of keying Carl's car or breaking some windows at the Shack. Even a mind as devious as his knew, however, that this destructive behavior was wrong. His pride was hurt worse than his rump when he fell to the sidewalk, drenched and with everyone laughing at him. *Oh, I'll get my revenge,* he thought, but in a way that would embarrass everybody at the Shack and at the same time make them wonder how someone had pulled it off undetected.

The plan Freddy had concocted was to sneak into the Shack late at night and cover the place in graffiti. He would paint the freezer, ice cream cooler, and the walls with choice vulgarities such as "fuck you Carl" and "eat me Donny." *Boy, that would teach those guys,* he thought. At first, he considered using spray paint but nixed that idea. Someone might see him buy it at the hardware store and it would be difficult for his uncle to remove. No, he'd use black and white shoe polish. His Mom kept an arsenal of that kind of stuff in the pantry and no one would miss the bottles he took. Some people might still suspect him as the culprit, but he'd leave no evidence or clues behind. Nobody would be able to figure out how he got into the building, either. *It would be the perfect crime,* he thought, *one that could never be solved!*

During his wet walk home on Friday, he wondered how Carl and Ron had gotten themselves up onto the roof. Freddy was a keenly observant young man and remembered something he had seen that answered his question. About a year ago, while riding his bike by the Action Corner, he'd watched a worker from the power company scale the backside of the Shack without a ladder, en route to trim back some tree branches that were close to power lines. It was the worker's last order of the day and, in hopes of finishing the small job quickly, the man skipped getting a ladder down from his truck and proceeded unaided. By standing on a nearby picnic table, grabbing a low-hanging branch, and then pivoting one foot against the tree trunk, the worker shimmied himself onto the building's lower roof, making it look easy.

Over the last couple years, Freddy had mastered the art of sneaking out late at night. He enjoyed the thrill of getting away with something that he knew he shouldn't be doing. He had memorized the location of all the crevices and dark spots between his house and the midway and could slink around the park undetected.

The night before the fire, he made a dry run at one in the morning to prove that he could vault himself onto the Shack's roof like he'd seen the lineman do. Despite his bulkiness, he'd already developed man-like arm strength and was surprisingly coordinated for his age. Arriving at the rear of the Shack, he hid his bike and executed the climbing maneuver flawlessly. Once on the roof, he was able to pry open one of the windows that hadn't been open in years. Peering into the dark upper floor, he figured this was all he needed tonight. *The rest of the job will be easy,* he thought. Confident that his plan would work, he went home.

All he needed to do from that point, then, was to gather up his supplies and wait. Everything would happen like clockwork, he thought. *Just like in the movies.*

After establishing that he could break into the building, Freddy moved on to the timetable for his deed. The Shack closed at midnight and he correctly surmised that Mel and his crew would be out of the building by 12:30. By that time, his mother and father would be sound asleep. Jimmy's regimented scheduled called for him to turn in by 11 every night. Diane was usually in an inebriated slumber by 10. His parents slept upstairs in a huge suite Jimmy had insisted on constructing once it was decided Freddy would be the only child. To accommodate this, Freddy moved into a bedroom on the first floor, essentially giving him exclusive use of the entire downstairs at night.

Saturday afternoon, Freddy moped around the house and took a nap before dinner. He found his Boy Scout knapsack and packed it with two bottles of shoe polish, a flashlight, and a bag of chocolate covered peanuts. He couldn't risk running out of energy in the middle of his mission.

At 12:45 a.m., his alarm clock went off with a muffled ring under his pillow. He got out of bed, already fully dressed, and crept outside the bedroom window to his bike, which he had pre-positioned earlier in the day. Freddy walked it a few steps away from the house, jumped on, and pedaled off into the night. He took his time going through the woods. During his ride, he did encounter a few partiers walking on the path, but nobody paid attention to him. *Just keep pedaling and act like you know what you're doing,* he said to himself. This had worked for him in the past; why would it be any different tonight? Freddy navigated his way through the trees and arrived at the backside of the Shack at 1:15. The last of the Lakeshore crowd had gone home and the midway was deserted.

He quickly scaled the building and gathered himself on the lower roof. The window opened much easier this time. Peering inside the tiny space, he groped in the darkness toward what he thought were steps down to his target area. Instead he found a large hole in the floor. He had no way of knowing it, but Mel had removed the staircase years ago to make way for a bigger potato room. In its place, Freddy saw a stepladder folded neatly against a wall below and out of his reach; he'd met his first unexpected challenge. Freddy paused for a moment to regroup and remembered the words he'd learned from his scoutmaster, Dutch, the very first day: *Be prepared.* Without hesitation, he mapped out an alternate route. Holding the flashlight between his teeth, he lowered himself into the staircase opening. His arms trembled from the strain, but he held on. He swung his feet back and forth until they found the top of the potato peeler. Gingerly, he eased himself onto the big metal tub and down to the floor, but lost his balance when his foot caught on something. He crashed down and lay on the cold cement. The flashlight fell out of his mouth, blinked a few times, and faded out. Freddy untangled his foot from whatever it was that caused him to trip; it felt like a bucket. He kicked it aside and cursed to himself. *Water bucket, stepladder to the roof; so that's how Carl and Ron had done it!* Bolstered with anger and determination, he pressed on.

He had never been inside the Shack, but knew its general layout from the outside. As he made his way toward the front counter, something seemed strange. It smelled like burning food inside. A bubbling sound rose above the hum of the refrigerators.

Freddy shook the flashlight and turned the switch on and off a few times, but no luck. *Darn! Why didn't I think to install new batteries before the mission?* he asked himself. He was pretty sure there were fluorescent ceiling lights on the windowless first floor, but was afraid to flip a wall switch, fearing that light might seep out through gaps in the wooden shutters. Remembering a scene from a war movie, he recalled how the platoon sergeant cautioned his men to "expect the unexpected," and so Freddy shifted gears. *There must be some matches near the grill,* he thought. As he felt his way in the darkness toward where he imagined the grill would be, he felt something splatter against his arm. It was hot and stung a little. Unfazed, he crept forward, bumping into what he thought was the hot dog grill. Slowly, he lowered his hands and felt a smooth metal surface. It was still warm.

He poked his hands under the grill, and sure enough came upon a box of stick matches. Smiling and full of himself now, Freddy lit a match, grabbed the black polish from his knapsack and went to work. He had just finished writing a big "F" on the refrigerator when the match burned down, scorching his fingertips. This wasn't going the way he had planned, but he was too far into the journey to give up now. After racking his brains for a while, he had a solution. He struck another match and found a stack of milkshake cups by the ice cream cooler. He stuffed one full of napkins and pulled a couple out the top to form a long paper fuse. Without thinking the next step through, Freddy held a match to the paper.

At first, his homemade torch worked fine. Freddy continued his writing spree, carefully tracing out a "U" when he felt another tingle against his arm. Looking down, he saw that he was standing next to one of the deep fryers. The oil inside was boiling. At this point, Freddy's adventure took a terrible turn. The cup and napkins began to burn more intensely. Flames rose to the ceiling and he panicked. Instinctively, he shook the torch, trying to put it out. A swatch of the burning paper flew off, landing squarely in the smoldering oil, and it ignited.

When Freddy had left the Boy Scouts, he hadn't learned about the different classes of fires and the dangers of mixing water with a flaming liquid. Now terrified, he filled another milkshake cup with water from the soda fountain and tossed it at the flames. The flare-up nearly knocked Freddy off his feet. Suddenly stacks of napkins and cups by the fryers caught on fire. Flames spread to the walls as sparks and burning oil erupted in all directions.

Freddy feared for his life. He bolted up the same route he had traveled before. Darkness was not a problem now. The inferno provided enough illumination for him to see his way as he scrambled up through the hatch and out the open window. He still wore the knapsack on his back, but couldn't remember if he'd grabbed the shoe polish or flashlight. At this point, he didn't care: all he wanted was to get the hell out of there. Gravity made his exit off the roof easier. He hopped on his bike and pedaled to a dark nook inside the midway.

At this point in his story, Freddy was no longer crying. His parents were so dumbfounded, neither thought of interrupting him. Finally Jimmy said, "Are you making this up?" The entire thing sounded like a fairy tale to him. His father's blunt question knocked Freddy back to reality. He had found a bizarre enjoyment telling the story and felt proud of himself for going undetected. He knew what a horrible mess he had caused, but his young mind couldn't grasp the penalty that could lie ahead for him.

As Diane listened to her son, she had no choice but to finally confront the fact of his incorrigible behavior. Her son was surrounded by a sort of evil energy. This was something that she, as his mother, couldn't comprehend. She had always hoped that eventually her son would come around and be more normal. If only she could go back to when Freddy was a baby and start over again.

From the time Freddy opened his mouth, Jimmy analyzed his every word. He quickly honed in on Freddy's description of the bubbling oil and deduced that, for whatever reason, a deep fryer was still on, overheating uncontrollably. Instead of dwelling on that moot point, Jimmy focused on every detail of his son's story. He had to know what he was up against if he were to put a lid on this thing.

As Freddy had sat cowering behind the Tilt-a-Whirl ride, he spotted Laparco taking his walk. Nearly an hour had passed since he escaped from the Shack and the initial flare-up had died down when the peanut oil burned out of the fryers. The fire still smoldered, however, and continued inching toward the reams of flammables Mel had bought for the weekend. Smoke stopped seeping from the building as Freddy watched the glow in the upper windows fade to barely a glimmer. *Maybe the fire is burning itself out*, he hoped.

Gradually he regained his courage, got up, and started walking alongside his bicycle, carefully staying in the shadows between amusement rides. He slowly made his way toward the canal edge and, seeing no one, heaved the knapsack with all his might. He heard a splash and sighed with relief, knowing that the rocks he put in for weight would carry the sack to the bottom. Turning from the water, he frowned when he realized that he had left his candy in the bag.

After walking a short distance back into the woods, Freddy got on his bicycle and pedaled away. About ten minutes had passed from the time he initially sighted Laparco and when he reached the end of the trail and rolled onto Main Street. He pulled his hooded sweatshirt up over his ball cap, praying that if anyone did seen him, they couldn't make out his face. The hood acted like a set of blinders, though, restricting his peripheral vision. When he crossed paths with Laparco, Freddy was pedaling as fast as he could, racing to get to his house. He never even saw Laparco running to pull the fire alarm.

The thrill of telling his story quickly wore off. Initially, Freddy was buoyed by adrenaline inundating his system as he talked, but when he finished and saw the horrified looks on his parents faces, he began sobbing again. Jimmy and Diane held a faint hope that none of this was really happening, but as outrageous as Freddy's story was, they both realized it was probably true.

The three of them sat silently for several minutes as Freddy waited for whatever his parents had in store for him.

Jimmy recognized that what he was about to say would have a major impact on his wife and son. With Diane speechless and in shock, Jimmy took the initiative.

"Freddy, this is terrible," he began. "What on earth gave you the right to break into another man's property!" Not waiting for a reply, he continued, "You could go to prison for doing this."

Freddy started to cry again, not knowing that as a juvenile, the law didn't allow him to be sentenced to jail time — reform school maybe, but not prison. Jimmy quickly gauged that any investigation would likely reveal how what started out as an unlawful prank had accidentally turned into a tragedy. Nonetheless, he had Freddy's total attention and needed to establish trust with him now.

"You must not say a word about this to anyone, do you understand me?" Jimmy leaned across the table and pointed a finger in Freddy's face. The boy nodded helplessly. "Your mother and I have to talk about this in private."

With that, Jimmy got his car keys and asked Diane to meet him outside. "Freddy, your mother and I are going for a ride. We'll be back in about an hour. Are you OK staying here alone?"

"Yes," Freddy said meekly.

"Remember, don't talk to anyone. Don't even answer the phone." Jimmy joined Diane who was already in the car. During their drive, he explained to her about his meeting with Mel. Jimmy now knew for sure that Mel wasn't bluffing. What concerned him the most, however, was how he could find out where the investigation was headed.

Were there any other witnesses? At that hour of the morning the amusement park and surrounding woods would have been deserted, but there was always a possibility someone else saw Freddy coming or going.

Jimmy's instincts told him he couldn't sit by idly and wait for things to happen. He had to be proactive.

"Barretti here." Jack answered his phone the same way he'd done since becoming a rookie trooper. He normally disdained office work but today it was a nice break from duty in the field. Besides, it was hot and humid outside and air conditioning had just been installed in the trooper headquarters that spring.

"Uh, hi Jack, this is Jimmy Rosco, calling from Woodland Beach."

Jack hesitated for a second. At first, he didn't connect the name with the face, and then mistakenly pictured Mel on the other end of the phone. Finally it all clicked and he replied, "Oh, hello Jimmy, it's been a while, hasn't it?"

"Over two years, actually," Jimmy answered. "Diane and I had a great time with you and your wife when we had dinner down in Florida."

Jimmy blushed at not remembering Mrs. Barretti's name. He hadn't started the conversation well and felt awkward; he was out of his element making small talk. He and Diane had had a chance encounter with the Barrettis at a restaurant in Florida.

Not knowing one another's names, but recognizing each other from back home, they had a few drinks and then sat together for dinner. The evening was cordial, but neither couple had felt the desire to follow up with any social activities since then.

After an uncomfortable silence, Barretti asked in his official voice, "What can I do for you today, sir?"

"That was quite a fire at my brother's place the other night, wasn't it?" Jimmy pressed on, now groping to get to his point.

"Yes, it was. I hope Mel and his family are doing well."

Jimmy ignored the officer's comments. "Any idea what happened?"

"Well, Jim, the matter is still under investigation." Barretti said deliberately. "The official report will be out soon and will become public knowledge at that time."

Again, there was an uncomfortable silence on the line. Jimmy realized that the conversation was going nowhere. "Oh, of course," he said. "I just wanted to thank your office for all the hard work you've done on the case. Please stop in at the Shoreline sometime for dinner, my treat."

"Thank you for the offer, Mr. Rosco. We aren't allowed to accept gratuities like that, but I sincerely appreciate it anyway."

"OK, Officer Barretti, you have a nice day now. Goodbye." Jimmy hung up the phone, never giving Barretti the chance to reply. He looked around his office and saw that the door was half open. He hoped none of the restaurant staff had overheard him.

On the other end of the line, Jack Barretti sat at his desk wondering, *What in the hell was that all about?*

Chapter Twenty-four

Mel and his family sat down at the dinner table. Rita had prepared stuffed bell peppers, one of the family's favorite meals. Normally they had simpler fare during the week. Stuffed peppers was a Sunday meal. This was Tuesday so the whole family was a little surprised when Rita served them.

"Wow!" Dickie said. His eyes twinkled at the sight of the steaming platter in front of him. Since the picnic at the Falls and the fireworks, there wasn't much for the family to look forward to, and Rita thought that a nice meal might cheer everyone up.

Until Laparco's revelation about Freddy, Mel had held onto the hope that the insurance claim would be paid promptly, allowing him and Rita to keep the creditors at bay for a while. The Roscos were just about broke, their income reduced to the meager few dollars Rita brought in from her job at the post office. Now, with his knowledge that a crime might have been committed, Mel feared that the whole matter would drag on. He planned to reopen the arcade this weekend, but its receipts wouldn't come close to covering their expenses.

The family said grace and started filling their plates when the phone rang.

"Now who could that be at dinner hour?" Rita said. She got up, shook her head with irritation and went into the kitchen to answer it. "Hello," she said. "Yes, this is the Roscos. Oh, hi Tom, how are you?"

Eating stopped as forks and knives dropped to the table. The family focused their attention on Rita, wondering who had called.

"Well, thank you for your concern. Yes, hold on, I'll get him for you."

"It's Tom Matson," Rita said in a whisper, covering the phone with her hand.

Tom Matson was a home builder from Elmira who had moved to North Carolina three years ago. He and his family had vacationed at the Beach for years before the move, and his oldest son, Tommy, had struck up a friendship with Donny Rosco when they both were ten years old. The two of them were like peas in a pod for three straight summers. They became such close friends that the last summer before moving south, Tommy stayed with the Roscos for two additional weeks after his family returned home. The Roscos and Matsons had gotten together a few times, going out for dinner or drinks during the summers. They continued to exchange Christmas greetings, but after the Matsons moved to Raleigh, the families hadn't seen or spoken to each other.

Tom Matson was a successful, wealthy developer, but he never forgot his humble roots. Throughout his life, he treated everyone with the same easygoing mannerisms as Mel and the two had looked forward to getting together every summer. But, in addition to their similar personalities, there was a bigger thing that kept their friendship alive over the years: they were both huge Yankee fans. When the Yanks were playing, neither one of them was more than ten feet from a radio.

Tom established himself quickly in the Raleigh home building scene. He was a go-getter, and despite his northern roots, the "good ol' boys" from North Carolina welcomed him into their fold when they realized he was a fair-minded businessman who shared their vision for the future of their community. Over three short years, Tom built up a solid team of tradesmen, bankers, and real estate agents. He and his family meshed well in their new town and Matson Builders was there to stay in North Carolina.

"Hey, Tom, how you doing?" Mel said. He beamed with the happiness of hearing from an old friend.

"We're all fine down here, Mel. I heard through some of our old neighbors up north about your fire. Sheila and I are so sorry for you guys," said Tom.

"Thanks, Tom," replied Mel. "It means a lot to hear that. We're hanging in there, though."

"That's good to hear. Listen, I know you're probably still reeling from what happened, but I have a proposition for you to think about. I don't know what your business plans are or if you're going to rebuild, but I could use another good man down here."

"Really, how's that?" Mel asked. Rita and the kids saw the astonishment on his face.

"I'm developing a new subdivision with plans for a second and third phase. I'm looking for someone to run our new sales office. I've always admired your way with people and I think you would do one heck of a job as my sales director."

"But Tom, I don't know much about building homes," Mel said with a nervous laugh.

"You don't have to. We can train you in a couple weeks on the basics. You'll have two other salesmen under you. I need someone I can trust, someone who puts people at ease when they come into the sales office. I've even got a vacant model for you and your family to live in for the time being. We'll work out the rent with your compensation package. Please think about it, Mel. We'd love to have you, Rita and the kids as neighbors."

"Tom, I don't know what to say," Mel said, still bowled over by the offer. All eyes were on him now. The family was hearing only one side of the conversation and they were ready to burst with curiosity. "Let me talk it over with Rita and the kids," he added.

"Sure, take some time. I know it would be a big move, but we've got some exciting things going on down here, and it would be great to have you part of it."

The two said their goodbyes and Mel hung up the phone.

At first, Mel didn't know how to explain his conversation, so he decided to simply repeat what Tom had said and not add any comments of his own. When he finished talking, Donny was the first to speak up.

"But Dad, why would we want to leave? This is where we live." Surprisingly, Rita and Sylvia were excited and teased each other about becoming Carolina belles as they feigned southern accents. Dickie listened to the discussion with mild interest, but focused on attacking his second stuffed pepper.

Mel sat back as the family took over the conversation. Although everyone at the table still thought of the Beach as their home, ever since the Shack fire it had been hard for them not to sense a change was brewing. Sure, friends would be missed, but there were no close family members in the area for them to leave behind. Rita's siblings lived out of state, and Jimmy, Diane, and Freddy were anything but close. Grandma Rosa would be missed, but they had less and less contact with her every year. She'd done a generous thing by raising Mel when his biological mother and father walked away, and Mel felt a lifelong indebtedness to her for that. After he reached adulthood, however, it seemed only natural for her to identify more with her true son Jimmy and his family. Mel held no expectations for his family members at the Beach.

After two hours of talking and eating, Rita asked her husband if he would take a walk with her. As the two of them left the house, the children's enthusiastic banter continued. The topic of discussion now turned to who would get the biggest bedroom at their new house.

It was a beautiful, warm summer evening as the sun sank slowly over the lake. The two of them walked casually down Park Avenue toward the midway. They said little during the half-mile stroll. The music and clatter from the amusement park grew in volume as they got closer and it lifted their spirits. That changed when the Shack came into view.

Nothing appeared to have changed since the fire Saturday night. Sadly, the sights and smells of the burned out hulk brought back the dreadfulness of it all over again. The two of them stood silently overlooking the ruins.

Mel spoke first. "You know, Rita, maybe it's time to move on. We've slugged it out here for over twenty years. I don't know why or how we would rebuild this place. We have so much debt, how could we ever dig ourselves out?"

Rita simply smiled and squeezed her husband's hand. No words could express how much she loved Mel at that moment. Mel saw it in her eyes and wanted to tell her everything about his conversations with Jimmy and Laparco. This was the first time in their marriage that he'd kept something of this magnitude from her. All evidence was pointing toward the fire being ruled an accident and he was afraid if he told anyone what he suspected had really happened, the whole issue would drag on forever. He and Rita expected that the insurance settlement would be enough to pay off the Shack's mortgage and provide a couple extra thousand dollars. Other than that, they had nothing. Their home was leveraged to the hilt and Mel had lost track of how much they owed suppliers.

Rita could tell the pain her husband was in. "Honey, your life has been a struggle ever since your mother left you on the doorstep. Rosa did her best to give you a normal life but it wasn't meant to be. Your brother will never change how he feels about you, and he'll always blame you for your father leaving. You're a good man, Mel; everyone at the Beach knows that. Tom Matson knows it too; that's why he called today and made you the offer."

She continued, "Sometimes God brings things into our lives that seem like tragedies. It knocks us down and shakes our very senses. I've prayed all week for a miracle, and it just came to our house tonight when the phone rang. I think Tom's call was a sign from above that it's time for a change."

Mel hung his head down and stared at the charred rubble in front of him. Tears began to well up in his eyes. A lifetime of disappointment and sorrow filled his heart, and would stay embedded there until he found a way to pull it out.

"Rita," he said, "You know that I love you with all that's in me and would do anything for you and the kids. I don't know why all this came into our lives, but it's here for a reason. I think I should call Tom back tomorrow and take the job."

Rita took his hand gently and touched it to her lips. She didn't have to say a word. Their decision was made.

Chapter Twenty-five

Jack Barretti stepped out of his sedan and was greeted by a swarm of bugs. He'd never driven back to this area of the Beach but surmised from the low level swamplands that it was the mother lode of mosquito havens. He walked briskly toward the house hoping to escape the onslaught of hungry insects.

Before he could knock on the door, he heard a frail voice from inside.

"He's out back," the woman said.

"Mrs. Wilcox, this is Jack Barretti with the state troopers. Is Carl at home?'

"Yes, he's out back," she said again. Jack wondered how the woman had guessed who he was or why he was here. *Probably the ugly colored car and the suit I'm wearing in this heat. Doubt if I'm the first cop to walk up this driveway,* Jack reasoned.

Barretti continued around the backside of the home and came upon a one car garage where he found Carl's big Buick, hood open and front end jacked up. A pair of legs stuck out from underneath.

"Carl Wilcox?" Jack hollered above the blaring music.

" Yup, who's there?" Carl answered. Carefully, he slid himself out from under the car. When he saw the cop hovering over him, Carl blanched, sat up on the creeper and began rubbing his hands nervously with a rag. He kept his eyes focused on cleaning his dirty hands as he stood up, leaned inside the car, and turned off the radio.

Before Carl could speak, the trooper introduced himself. "I'm officer Jack Barretti with the BCI. I've been assigned the duty of investigating the Shack fire. Mind if I ask you some questions?"

"Sure," Carl said. He finished cleaning his hands and set the rag down on his work bench. Barretti noticed how immaculate the shop was. The rest of the property was a disaster; the house desperately needed painting and the yard was strewn with old tires, lumber, and what not. Inside the garage, though, not a single item was out of place.

A car tinkerer himself, Jack couldn't help but break from formality to comment.

"Nice shop."

"Thanks," Carl replied. He was surprised that the big cop would notice.

"Can you tell me what you did after leaving work Saturday night, the second?

"Well, me and my buds, Ron and Ollie, helped Mel close up around 12:30, and then drove to a beach party on the north shore. Stayed there 'til dawn."

Barretti made some notes in a small green notebook the force had issued him.

"Any thing look suspicious when you closed up and left?"

"Naw, it was business as usual for us. We worked our asses . . . sorry . . . we put in a long day and just wanted to unwind. The three of us headed over to Ollie's to clean up before the party."

"Notice anyone around the building when you left?"

"Yeah, the place was crawlin' with people from the Lakeshore letting out. Some were walking between the Shack and Mel's arcade going to their cars."

"OK, fine," Barretti said, making a few more notes. He'd already interviewed Ollie and Ron and their stories matched up. Ollie's father had confirmed that the boys were outside showering around one.

"Did you happen to see any of the Lakeshore employees or midway people anywhere near the Shack when you left?"

"Yeah, actually now that you mention it, I did see Willis and Laparco carrying some garbage out to the trash cans by the parking lot." Carl thought for a minute and asked, "Do you think one of them did it?"

Barretti ignored the question and tucked the notebook in his breast pocket. He felt sweat seeping through his dress shirt.

"Thanks for your time, Mr. Wilcox." Barretti extended his hand to Carl and shook it firmly. "This car of yours is pretty famous around the barracks, did you know that?"

Carl reddened at Barretti's words. He'd hoped that his reputation wouldn't come up. Not knowing how to reply, he just stood there and looked at Barretti with a guilty face.

"Carl, I got something I want to say off the record," Barretti said, still gripping his hand. "By the looks of this car and seeing how you keep your shop, you got a lot of potential, son. It'd be a terrible waste of talent if you spend the rest of your life drag racing and sitting on your ass drinking beer. We got enough street punks around here already."

Carl wasn't sure where this was leading and he wished that Barrreti would loosen his grip; it was starting to hurt. He stood firm however, refusing to show the pain. He figured the cop was about to give him a ticket for something.

Barretti finally drew his hand away, took out his notebook again and began writing. "I imagine you have plenty of free time now that the Shack is gone. Here's a number to call. My brother-in-law runs the barracks garage and I hear he's always looking for good mechanics."

"Thanks, officer," Carl said. He breathed a sigh of relief. This was the last thing he would have expected from the cop. He took the paper and tacked it on the wall next to a girlie calendar.

"Slow down a little, son, or you're gonna lose your license," Barretti said over his shoulder. "It's tough getting to work when you have to walk."

The phone rang at 9 a.m. sharp. It was Phil Graff from the insurance office.

"Mel, it looks like the investigation is finalizing on all ends. The county inspectors submitted their report last evening and Jack Barretti just called to tell me he was driving over today to give me a copy of his report. Can you stop by after lunch so we can go over everything?"

Mel was surprised that things were progressing so quickly. It had only been a few days since the fire. All parties had implied, however, that they would do their best to expedite the investigation so the insurance claim could proceed and Mel could rebuild. All these people were going the extra distance to pave the way for him. By picking up and moving, Mel felt he was turning his back on everyone. The line grew quiet as Phil waited for a reply. Finally Mel answered, "Sure, Phil, I'll see you around one if that's OK."

Jimmy Rosco decided not to seek out more information about the fire. His attempt to pry some facts from Barretti had been embarrassing and he was savvy enough to know any further talking might tip off someone about what he knew. Jimmy wasn't comfortable operating in such a vacuum. Panic was not an emotion he dealt with often, but when he did, he normally powered through it. While talking with Barretti, though, he heard fearfulness in his own voice.

Barretti attributed Jimmy's strange phone call to nervousness. Experience showed him that most people were out of their element when conversing with a lawman. Psychopaths and hardened criminals could master the art of deception but not the average guy. Barretti concluded that Mel Rosco's brother was merely curious and felt that their previous social contact in Florida gave him the liberty to make such a call. There was no reason for the BCI officer to think otherwise.

Freddy and Diane went about their normal daily routines. Actually, Freddy felt a huge sense of relief at having confessed. He was too young and immature, however, to fully comprehend the gravity of the situation. Right now, he was content to stay quiet and let his father handle it. Oddly, Diane and Jimmy had no further discussion of the issue with their son, and Diane said little to her husband about it as she decided to put her trust in his judgment. Jimmy always steered the family on the right course, she rationalized.

When Mel arrived at the insurance office, Phil was seated at his desk with a load of folders in front of him. "Good Lord, this paperwork gets longer and longer. Look at this stuff: fire inspectors, police reports, Chief Johnson's summary. If I got paid by the sheet, I'd be a millionaire!" Phil said. Mel gave a polite smile, appreciating Phil's attempt to lighten the mood.

"Well, looks like we're going to rule the fire as an accident caused by a faulty deep fryer thermostat." Phil peered over the top of his reading glasses at Mel. "Your annual inspections are all valid and there's no evidence of foul play. Barretti's initial suspicions of Anthony Laparco's involvement were dispelled by the timeline of the fire. Both Willis Shank and Steve Mills gave statements corroborating that Laparco was in his room sleeping until nearly 3 a.m. The county inspectors are convinced that the fire was burning for at least one to two hours before the fire trucks responded. Mel, my company is ready to cut you a check as early as next week. I'll personally drive this report to our regional office in Syracuse tomorrow to speed things up."

Mel sat still for a few seconds, glancing at the pile of folders and reports on the agent's desk. Nearly all of his life's accomplishments had been reduced to pile of rubble a few miles away and a stack of paper on Phil's desk. In his heart, though, Mel felt a sense of hope. Tom Matson's call yesterday had buoyed him and Rita at their lowest moment.

"You OK?" Phil asked.

"Yeah I'm fine, Phil, just a little overwhelmed by it all."

Phil paused before continuing. "Mel, I've been doing this work for a long time. I've watched how catastrophes can knock people down. Some never get back up. Others do, but never get past the 'what ifs,' hoping that everything will go back to the way it was before. And then sometimes it's as if the setback forces people to reach down deep within themselves and find the strength to move forward in a direction they never would have imagined. I've known you and Rita for your entire marriage. You two are solid people and have three great kids. I think that your best years are still ahead of you."

Mel knew that Phil was right: he *was* blessed with a terrific wife and beautiful children. The fire could never destroy that. It would be tough for them to leave, but Mel knew in his heart it had to be.

When Mel got home, the house was empty. Rita was still at work and Sylvia had left a note that her boyfriend John had come by and taken her, Donny, and Dickie for a drive in his new car. The kid had purchased a 1939 Ford sedan from a farmer who'd parked the broken vehicle alongside his barn, where it had sat for years. John had agreed to pay the man only if he was able to get the car running and drive it off the property, which after three weeks of tinkering, he did. The old-timer stood amazed at the sight of the clunker idling in his driveway. John proudly counted out the agreed upon price, one hundred, and drove straight to the Beach to show off his prize.

Mel made a fresh pot of coffee and sat down to digest the week's events. Last Friday his thoughts had been immersed in the anticipation of a Golden Weekend. About the only thing he cared about at that time was to have four decent days of business and to catch up on his debts. Instead, he had witnessed his livelihood disappear and was on the verge of moving his family to a place he'd never been. *Is this all really happening or am I dreaming?* he asked himself.

The weekend dragged on as Mel and his family searched for a way to get on with their lives. His half-hearted attempt to reopen the arcade proved to be a bust when a big storm blew through, and the midway became a ghost town.

After three hours at the arcade, Mel took in less than two dollars in profits. It was never that dismal at the Shack, even when the weather was lousy. Frustrated and dejected, he closed the doors and went home.

Over the weekend he and Rita held a family meeting with the kids. The initial euphoria ebbed and tears began to flow as the stark realities of moving set in. Mel explained to the kids how he felt this was an opportunity the family had to take and they couldn't back down now. Despite their sadness, everyone agreed.

Phil Graff called Monday afternoon and delivered the news that Mel's settlement check was ready. He and Rita had been up most of the night working out some numbers and planning what to do with the money. They had never seen the amount of money they anticipated from the payout and didn't know where to begin. Eventually, they formulated a plan.

First, they would make a proposition to the bank: Mel would sell whatever items were salvageable from the fire, haul away the remaining rubble and offer to turn over the vacant land to the bank in return for forgiveness of the three mortgages against the property. They felt that the property had substantial value on its own and hoped that the bank agreed with them. Next, they would pay off back taxes and settle up with the suppliers and equipment companies they owed. This would consume the lion's share of the settlement. Finally, all employees, including Sylvia, Donny, and Dickie, would receive the wages they were due. Any money left after that would help fund their move to North Carolina.

There were a lot of variables and unknowns to the plan and it certainly wasn't bulletproof; nonetheless, it was the best solution they could come up with.

Chapter Twenty-six

Jimmy Rosco hadn't slept more than a few hours at a time since meeting with Mel at the stone barn. As cool a businessman as he was, his knowledge of Freddy's involvement with the fire was tearing at his conscience. The purely truthful thing for him to do, he thought, would be to come forward, bring Freddy to the BCI office and let the cards fall where they may. If Freddy's story was accurate, there was a fair chance that a judge would view the whole thing as a reckless adolescent prank gone wrong. Freddy would have to suffer the consequences, but he was a minor and Jimmy assumed that the likelihood of a first time offender being sentenced to a juvenile facility was low. What concerned him more, however, was how such a scandal would affect his and Diane's status in the community. The town placed them on a pedestal and, ironically, Jimmy's cold aloofness created a mystique that further enhanced their position. Most people respected Jimmy Rosco and some even feared him. The local politicians, bankers and other merchants always turned to him to gauge how the community was doing.

Yes, Jimmy knew the right thing to do. He also knew he didn't have the guts to do it. Confident that doing nothing was his wisest path, he chose to ride it out and hope for the best.

There was an unknown wild card, however, that continued to gnaw at him: if Mel wanted to go to the police, why hadn't he already done so? Was he waiting for Jimmy to approach him with hush money?

Jimmy might be able to lay low with everyone else, but not with his brother. He had to talk to Mel again.

"I wish we could have done better for you Mel. I know this won't make things the way they were, but it's a start." Phil Graff handed Mel an envelope containing the settlement check.

Mel opened it — twelve thousand, nine hundred dollars. Not quite what he and Rita had estimated, but it would have to do. Phil continued to rattle on with insurance jargon: depreciation, replacement costs, deductibles, fair market value. . . . Mel politely gave the appearance of paying attention but his mind was elsewhere. He felt awkward and just wanted to take the money and go home. Phil saw it all over Mel's face and mercifully wrapped up his remarks.

The insurance man had done this dozens of times over the years and always had the same hollow feeling when he handed over a check. There was no way in hell that a piece of paper with numbers on it was going to return someone's life to the way it was before an accident or fire.

"Take care, Mel," Phil said.

Mel tucked the check in his shirt pocket and headed for the door.

"OK Phil, you too."

Jimmy sat alone in his office for over an hour, thinking out his next move. Finally, he called in his day manager.

"Tony, would you take this pie over to my brother's house? I'll stay here and fill in for you." Jimmy had boxed up a fresh banana cream pie to send over to Mel's. "Oh, and take this with you too, will ya?"

He handed Tony a sealed envelope that had "Mel" printed on it. Jimmy didn't want to call on the phone. He had seen Rita earlier at the post office and took the chance that Mel would be the one to answer the door when Tony knocked. Inside the envelope was a note that read, "We need to talk again. Meet me at the same place at 2 p.m."

Tony hopped into his car for the short drive. As expected, Mel answered the door and the two men exchanged pleasantries. Mel walked back to the kitchen and opened the pie box before the envelope. He loved banana cream pie and had to admit Jimmy's was the best around. Still, it was odd for Jimmy to extend any gesture of friendship like this toward his brother. As Mel opened the envelope, Jimmy's blunt request chilled any warmth the gift had conveyed.

By the time of their rendezvous at the stone barn, a light rain had begun to fall. Jimmy got there first and motioned for Mel to join him inside his car. Reluctantly, Mel did. He would have preferred staying outside, but the weather was getting ugly and it made sense to take cover.

"So how was your Fourth?" Mel asked as he slid into the leather seat of Jimmy's Cadillac.

"Not bad. About what we expected," Jimmy answered matter-of-factly. He wasn't quite sure where Mel's small talk was leading and kept up his guard.

"Actually, mine was wonderful, Jim. I spent it with my family and we watched the fireworks together. I've had a nice little vacation the last few days . . ."

"Cut the crap, Mel. I don't know where this is going and I don't have the time. What's it going to take to keep everybody quiet?"

"What?"

"You know what I mean, how much money?" Jimmy turned his head and gazed out the window. A thunderstorm was rolling in off the lake and rain came down in sheets now.

Mel sat there, disgusted. "So that's what this is about, huh?"

"I know what happened to your place and I'm willing to make your life a lot easier if we can all put a lid on this. I got one favor to ask, though. You have to figure a way to shut up that moron Laparco. He's the only one who has a chance of pinning this on Freddy. Do you have any idea what this will do to me if it gets out?"

Mel shook his head in disbelief. "What this will do to you? Are you serious? Whose business was destroyed, Jimmy? Rita and I are about ready to move into the poorhouse and you're worried about you. Nothing ever changes, does it?"

"What's your price, Mel?"

"You gotta be kidding. That's why you asked me up here?"

Jimmy didn't know what to say. Rain pelted the roof of the car and the air inside grew humid. He broke out in a nervous sweat.

"Have you ever thought about what the words family or loyalty really mean?" Mel went on. "For the record, Anthony Laparco didn't go to the cops after seeing Freddy Saturday night; he came to me, somebody he could trust. That guy may be a little off upstairs, but he actually thinks he's doing the right thing keeping the law away from Freddy because you're my brother.

Nobody else knows where Freddy was that morning and you can thank Anthony Laparco for that."

Jimmy felt as if someone had knocked his legs out from under him. After the disastrous conversation with Barretti he'd made a vow never to lose control of a situation again, but Mel's truths cut him to the quick and he was defenseless.

"Where were you when I really needed you, Jimmy? This has been going on our whole lives and I'm sick of it. You always hated me because you thought it was my fault that Dad left. You never included me in your life or welcomed my family into your home. And now you're ready to buy me off to protect the pathetic mess you call your life. Your wife is a drunk and your son crying for help. I pity you, Jimmy, I really do."

Unfazed, Jimmy persisted. "Take this. You're going to need it." He held out an envelope stuffed with hundred dollar bills. "It's ten grand, that's all I can round up now." Mel saw the coldness in his brother's eyes. This was business now, and Jimmy was back on familiar ground.

Mel looked at the money and then back up at Jimmy. His whole life he'd held on to the belief that maybe someday it would be different. Sadly, the look on Jimmy's face erased any hopes that things would ever change.

"I don't want your money, Jimmy. Can't you see, all I ever wanted was to be your brother. That's all. But I was never good enough. I just got in your way."

Mel reached into his pocket. "Here, we found this on the floor of the Shack. I think you know who it belongs to." He placed the small, blackened flashlight on the dash. At first, Jimmy wasn't sure what it was, but after picking it up and seeing the Scouts emblem and engraved name, he knew. He understood that this was probably the only real evidence that could tie Freddy to the fire, and now his brother was turning it over to him.

"Do something to help your son before its too late," Mel said. He got out and walked to his truck. The storm front had passed and the rain settled into a light drizzle. As he drove away he looked over at the Cadillac. He saw Jimmy staring back at him, expressionless; he still held the money in one hand and the flashlight in the other.

Chapter Twenty-seven

When Mel returned home, Rita was there but the kids were gone. As he walked in, he heard the washing machine running and saw his wife folding clothes on the kitchen table. Rita could tell immediately how upset her husband was.

"What's wrong, honey?" she asked. Mel fought back the emotions that wanted to burst out of him. Things were happening so fast, and he struggled to keep his composure, but he had to stand tall now. His family needed him.

"Rita, do you know how long the kids will be gone?"

"They should be home in a couple of hours. John took them out for a drive in his new car and when the storm hit, they ducked into his place. Syl called and said John's mother invited them all for dinner."

Mel looked at the kitchen clock. It read 4:35.

"Sit down. I've got something I need to talk to you about." Initially, Mel had hoped to keep the news of Freddy's involvement to himself. He planned to tell Rita eventually when he had time to work it all out in his head, but this couldn't wait any longer.

"I'm sorry that I didn't share this with you sooner, but I thought it would be best if left until later. Now you deserve to know everything," Mel began.

He retraced the story, beginning with his meeting with Laparco after the fire. Mel then went into detail about the opened window he'd discovered, the flashlight, and his rendezvous with Jimmy at the stone barn. Rita started to cry as he relayed the incredible chain of events that had altered their lives forever.

At first, she was furious at him for not involving her earlier, but as he explained his reasons, the anger subsided. Mel told her how he felt sorry for Freddy and the way Jimmy and Diane had ignored the kid, and that when he had learned Freddy had something to do with the fire, he just couldn't bring himself to go to the police.

Nonetheless, it bordered on surreal how the kid had stumbled through the whole thing and, in the end, no one else could piece it together. Not the investigators, Jack Barretti, or the insurance agent. The two key elements of the crime, Laparco's testimony and Freddy's flashlight, would never be brought into play unless someone chose to come forward. Jimmy now held one half of the puzzle, the flashlight, and Anthony Laparco held the other. Mel couldn't fathom why Laparco might speak up at this point, but knew even if he did, his revelations would sound like a fantasy concocted by someone the town considered a half-wit.

The way Mel saw it, he and Rita should cash the insurance check and take the job in North Carolina. Yes, there was deceit involved, but what good would come to anybody if the secret were exposed? Enough damage had been done and enough lives were scarred forever. *No*, Mel reasoned, *let it stand as is.*

Rita gathered her thoughts and spoke. "Mel, you'll have to be the one to make the decision," she said. "I am so mad with your brother and his family for all the years of disrespect and abuse they heaped on us and now for Freddy to get away with this — it's so wrong!" The strain of the last week finally got the best of her as her head sunk to the table and tears flowed uncontrollably.

"I know, Rita," Mel said as he rubbed her head softly. "These last few days have opened my eyes to a lot of things. I never felt like I had much of a family growing up. Rosa did the best she could for me and I will always love her for that but I can never change the way Jimmy feels about me. And besides, if we go to the cops, what good is that going to do? We won't get any more money from the claim unless we take Freddy to court. Do you really want to go through all of that?" Mel was pleading with his wife now. They had always been able to discuss their problems on good terms, without egos getting in the way, but nothing like this had ever crossed their path before.

Mel saw the love in his wife's swollen eyes. He knew she felt the same way he did.

"Honey, I trust your instincts about this," she said. "What's done is done. Let's move on."

Mel called Tom Matson the next day to accept the job. They agreed to hold off planning the move for a couple weeks. He and Rita needed time to settle their affairs and prepare for the first major move of their lives. Other than the small apartment they'd lived in until Sylvia was two, this was the only home they'd known.

The first week of August arrived and as Steve Mills proclaimed every year at that time, "It's all over." By this he meant, "I know there's still plenty of summer left, but the hottest, busiest, and most exciting days of the season are behind us." He was right. The evenings were a little cooler, the sunsets a little earlier, and folks started to think of what their lives would be like after Labor Day.

What little could be salvaged from the Shack was auctioned off. The rest of the debris was loaded into three Dumpsters and hauled away. Mel and Donny were the only family members on hand when the demolition crew finished the clean up. Carl drove by to say hello but, other than that, it was business as usual at the Beach. The amusement rides spun and gyrated, the joints rocked and rolled, and teenagers made out on the shore at night. When the last scooper full of debris was loaded, all that remained behind was a sixteen by twenty concrete slab and four decades of memories.

Mel and Donny stood in the middle of the vacant lot and glanced around them. Neither said a word. Donny looked at his dad's face and could see the pain of a man who was fighting valiantly to keep his heart from being ripped out. All the hard work and sacrifices of building a business, and now it was gone. As the trucks hauled away the last remains of the Shack, it struck Donny that this place had been more than the wood, nails, and junk that was headed for the landfill. The trucks would dump their load and the material would go back into the earth where it came from, but the laughter and memories of the Shack would go on forever. Donny Rosco didn't know it at the time, but this was his first realization of what life really meant. He always wondered what gave his dad the strength and determination to go on when things got tough. Now he knew the answer: it was the human spirit and the faith that everything in our lives has a purpose. *There's a reason for all this to be happening*, he thought.

As Donny looked at Mel, he saw a peaceful smile come over his father's face. It was if the man were saying, "OK, God, this was miserable what you put on my plate, but I'll keep going, as long as you keep pulling me along."

Mel turned to see his son was looking at him. He put his arm around Donny's shoulder and said, "Come on, kiddo, there's nothing for us here anymore. Let's go home."

Rita and Mel carried out their plan and successfully negotiated with the creditors, allowing them to leave the Beach with a clean financial slate. The bank encouraged Mel to rebuild but more out of nostalgia than good business sense. One of the bank vice-presidents had actually worked at the Shack in the '40s and commented that the Beach would never be the same without the place. Like everyone, he raved about the old style french fries cooked in peanut oil. Ironically the very things that put the Shack on the map were in fact the source of its destruction: the ancient deep fryers were on their way to a final resting place at the village dump.

As the move drew closer, one by one the family said their goodbyes. Rita's girlfriends at the post office threw her a surprise party and the two boys made the rounds on their bikes to say so long to their pals. Probably the most difficult goodbye was Sylvia's to her boyfriend John. They were both seventeen and entering their junior year of high school. Dreams of football pep rallies, Sadie Hawkins dances, and the junior prom were put on hold. The two young adults vowed to write every week and Sylvia promised to travel north next summer to visit. People came to say goodbye and Mel invited them inside to sit and reminisce. No one could really believe that Mel and Rita were leaving.

Chapter Twenty-eight

Mel reached over to turn off the alarm clock before it rang. Rita had set it for 7 a.m. but it was only 5:30 and he was already wide awake. They had stayed up until after midnight, both nervous about the move today. Rita was in a deep sleep as Mel quietly got dressed. He skipped his morning ritual of making coffee and went outside. It was still dark and, other than a few early risers going to work, the streets were deserted.

Rosa Rosco was the only person Mel had deliberately avoided since the fire. Whenever she called or stopped by, he always had things to do and made it a point to change the subject when she asked him or Rita about their plans. Eventually, Rosa gave up asking, and although hurt, she respected her stepson's wish for privacy.

It was a mile and a half to Rosa's house and Mel thought the walk might feel good. The cool morning air helped clear his head. He wasn't sure what he would say, but he knew that he couldn't leave without spending some private time with the woman who had raised him. As he approached the house, the aroma of fresh coffee drifting from the kitchen window greeted him. All those years of working two or three jobs had conditioned Rosa to wake before dawn; most of the house lights were on and she was already dressed. Before he could knock, she met him at the door, a hot cup of coffee in each hand.

"Morning, Rosa," Mel said. He'd stopped calling her "Mom" when in his teens. Jimmy's repeated glares had made him self-conscious about using the word.

"Well, good morning to you too, stranger. I was wondering if you were going to come by at some point before you left. Wasn't exactly expecting visitors before sunrise but come on in," she said.

Mel noticed a large flowerpot on the porch. Inside was a withered, greenish-brown plant.

"I think your flowers need some water."

"Oh, that! Your Aunt Sophie is trying to convert me into a gardener. She dug it up when I was there on the Fourth. Believe it or not, it's a tomato plant."

"Could have fooled me," Mel replied.

"Well, I guess one green thumb in the family is enough." They both laughed, visualizing Sophie's antics in her beloved garden.

"Yeah, I remember the cases of vegetables and sauce she and Al hauled up to us every year. Nothing like home grown, huh?" Mel waited for Rosa to respond but she was silent and the polite smile had left her face. He knew she could read him like a book and knew he wasn't here to make small talk.

"I didn't really come by at this hour to talk about gardening, Rosa. I wanted to see you before the movers come today. Things have been happening so fast since the fire."

Rosa studied the face of the man she had known for nearly forty years. After an awkward silence, she spoke up.

"Mel, why are you really leaving the Beach? Everyone knows this is where your heart is. There's more to all of this than meets the eye, isn't there? I tried talking to your brother about it, but he clams up just like you. You two might fool everyone else but not your mother. What exactly hap—"

"Rosa, just let it be, please," Mel said, interrupting her. "It's too late for any of us to turn back now. Someday maybe you'll understand, but it's time for Rita and me to go. No, it won't be easy. But we can't stay."

"But why not? If it's a money thing, I can talk to Jimmy and see if he'll help you rebuild the Shack. I know you two don't get along, but he is your brother." The calmness had left her voice; she was pleading with him now.

Mel gently put his hands on her shoulders. She looked old and tired, and not like the little dynamo he remembered growing up. He wanted so badly to tell her the truth but knew it would only make things worse.

"No," he said flatly. Rosa knew that once Mel made his mind up, there was no changing it.

"Your son, your *real* son and his family are going to need you more than you will ever know. I love you for all that you have done for me and the sacrifices you've made to give me a home, but I have to go it alone now. If we stay here, I'll always be in Jimmy's shadow. No one should have to live like that."

Rosa hugged him. "I understand how you feel, Mel. I wish I could make things different but I can't. I'm going to miss you, Rita, and the kids so much." She hugged him tightly and remembered all the joy he'd brought into her life. *If only my own son could be like this,* she thought.

"Rosa, you were a better mother to me than any woman could have ever been," Mel said. He felt her body heave with sadness as she held him. For a brief moment, he was safe again as a child and didn't want to pull away, but slowly he did. He had to clear his throat to make the lump go away.

"Hey, now you got an excuse to get out of the cold and come visit us in the winter," he said, hoping to lighten the mood. "Come see us for Christmas, OK?"

Rosa wiped the tears from her eyes and gave him one final hug as he started to leave. "Mel, don't forget to honk your horn when you cross the state line tonight."

"Yeah, I know." He got a sudden case of the giggles remembering all the trips to Sophie's. "Welcome to Pennsylvania!" he said loudly as he walked across the lawn.

"The Keeeeeystone State!" Rosa shouted back.

When the moving van appeared, the stark reality of the event hit the family hard. They had all been busy and excited preparing for the change, but the actual thought of the move was just a spot on the horizon. When Rita looked up from packing the last of the kitchenware to see the van, an involuntary gasp came from her lips. The truck's diesel engine rumbled softly as the doorbell rang.

"Mrs. Rosco?" asked the man.

"Yes?"

"Stan Polski from Newark. You folks ready to start?" The short, stocky man had half an unlit cigar poking out from the side of his mouth. A large roll of inventory stickers was in one hand and a clipboard rested under his arm. Rita was speechless and searched for some words to say. She had only moved twice in her entire life. The first time was from the house where she grew up into the small apartment she and Mel rented when they married. The second time was when she and her husband bought the house they were now in. Other than a few trips to see relatives in Pennsylvania, she had spent her thirty-eight years within a fifty-mile radius of where she was born.

Tom Matson had bartered a favor from the owner of a New Jersey moving company who had bought one of his homes for retirement. The agreement was, if the Roscos would box and package their household goods, the moving company would load and drive the shipment from door to door, free of charge.

The Roscos would move into a brand new home, sight unseen. Tom sent a few snapshots and a brochure with a layout of the floor plan. The house itself looked nice in the pictures, but the land around it appeared barren and muddy. Instead of grass and trees, mounds of dirt and construction equipment surrounded the building.

Tom offered Mel and his family three months of free rent. From that point, after Rita found a job and Mel was a full time employee of Matson Builders, they could rent with an option to buy. All of the rent would be credited to the purchase price. It was obvious that Tom wanted to make this a sweet deal for the Roscos. His motives weren't based solely on friendship, though the Matsons and Roscos thought the world of each other. Tom Matson was a smart businessman and understood that people like Mel and Rita would spread the word to other folks up north if they liked their new home. Word of mouth was his most effective means of advertising.

"So, you Yankees ready to be surrounded by rednecks down in Carolina?" Stan asked as he began to place stickers on boxes and fill out his inventory sheets. The cigar stub bobbled up and down as he spoke, appearing to be hinged on his mouth.

"Oh, I hope we're not surrounded by rednecks," said Rita, not knowing if this brash Jersey guy was serious.

"Nah, nice people down there, and Mr. Matson is a favorite of ours. We do a lot of moves into his developments and I think you'll be happy."

Stan then launched into a detailed account of how he and his partner had been on the road for over two weeks and how much he missed his wife's home cooking. He had three kids, the oldest serving in the Army in Vietnam, and a boy and girl in high school. He would have continued on with his life story had Sylvia not interrupted to ask her mom whether she should pack her makeup kit or carry it with them in the car. Stan nodded and proceeded on with his work.

Mel, Donny, and Dickie offered to help the two man crew but they were pros and said "thanks but no thanks." They had a system and worked better alone. By 4:30 the last of the furniture was on board the big truck. The boys marveled at how much stuff could be packed so tightly. The Roscos' entire world filled up just over half the van.

Stan proudly explained that if every item was packed tight and secure, there would be less chance of damage due to shifting during the drive. He had been loading and driving for over twenty years and boasted, "There ain't nothing I don't know about the moving business." As the crew finished up, Rita brought out a pot of chili she had cooked over at a neighbor's house; all of her kitchen utensils were packed and her neighbor had graciously offered the use of her kitchen. The two movers were touched as she ladled out the chili and thanked her for taking the time. Dickie and Donny joined them onboard the truck and the group ate their meal using cardboard boxes as tables.

Mel was busy inside filling an envelope with directions and a spare map the movers had given him. As he folded up the papers, he saw Laparco standing in the kitchen doorway.

"Hey, Anthony! Nice of you to stop by," Mel said. He was one of the few people who called Laparco by his proper name; never Tony, always Anthony.

"You're really leaving, aren't you, Mel?" Laparco asked. He rubbed his hands nervously against his pants pockets.

"Guess so, my man," Mel answered. He could see that Laparco was having a hard time saying what he wanted to say. Mel tried to help by speaking first.

"How about you and me taking a little walk along the beach?"

"Sure, whatever you say." Laparco seemed glad to leave the empty house. They walked the two blocks from Mel's house to the waterfront and both took their shoes off when they got to the sand.

"I won't tell anyone, I promise," Laparco blurted out unexpectedly. Mel glanced around. There was no one within two hundred feet of them. It was midweek and the season truly was winding down. Not "over" as Steve had pronounced, but noticeably slower.

"Anthony, the last thing I would ever want you to do for me or anyone else would be to lie," Mel began. "That night of the fire, I'm pretty sure you did see Freddy riding his bike, but the official report shows that the fire was an accident. One of the deep fryers overheated and once the flames got going, the place never had a prayer. If anyone ever asks you if you saw Freddy that night, you tell them the truth. But as far as my family, and my brother and his family are concerned, the fire was an accident. You are a great friend, Anthony. Rita and I will always welcome you into our home, no matter where we live."

Laparco was fighting back tears as he extended his hand. Mel grabbed his hand and pulled his friend into a big bear hug.

"You take care of yourself, OK, partner?" he said. Laparco didn't answer but simply nodded his head as the two men parted. After leaving Rosa's earlier, Mel thought he'd said the last of the sad goodbyes, but this one wasn't much easier.

Mel started walking back to his house as Laparco turned and headed in the direction of the Lakeshore. After a few steps they turned simultaneously. Mel smiled and gave him a salute. Laparco returned a toothy grin and waved back.

Mel Rosco and Anthony Laparco would never see each other again.

Chapter Twenty-nine

"Ladies and gentlemen, we will be landing in Syracuse in approximately ten minutes. Please check that your seatbacks and tray tables are in their full upright positions." The lead flight attendant finished the announcement and then joined the rest of her crew as they prepared the cabin for landing.

Donny Rosco checked his watch: 4:30, right on time. His flight from Tampa via Charlotte had gone smoothly and he was able to get some paperwork done en route. Since starting with the In-Tech software company after college he'd advanced through the company, starting as a software writer and now heading its engineering and development division. The family had moved south seventeen years ago, and other than a trip back to attend Rosa's funeral in 1972 after her sudden passing, Donny hadn't returned to his hometown. This was the first time he'd seen the area from the air. It was a breathtaking sight and he was enthralled with its natural beauty of lush rolling hills and farmland on this late June afternoon. Scanning the horizon, he finally got his bearings and found what he was looking for, Indian Lake. It appeared bigger than he'd imagined and he had to put on his glasses to focus in on the east end of the lake. He could make out Woodland Beach's famous stretch of sand spanning the entire eastern shore.

As the plane taxied to the gate, Donny couldn't help but remember the events that had transpired after leaving New York. The move to Raleigh turned out to be a great thing for the family, although not without its problems. After the initial euphoria of the change wore off, the reality of being uprooted set in with each of them in their own way. Rita spent days crying and missed the ladies from the post office. It took three months for her to make a real friend in the neighborhood. While preparing Thanksgiving dinner the day before the holiday, a woman three houses down the street sheepishly knocked on Rita's door hoping to borrow some sugar. The women chuckled when they realized neither was a native Southerner as each had suspected. As time went on, the Roscos met more and more folks transplanted from "up north."

Sylvia went through a difficult time as the new girl in school. Her beauty and congeniality was a natural magnet to attract the boys, but this served as a hurdle to her becoming friends with her female classmates. Undaunted, Syl pressed on, volunteering to help everyone and anyone who needed it. She joined the drama club, and slowly the ice that held the girlish high school cliques together began to melt. By the end of her junior year she was liked and respected by most everyone in her school. Her kind heart and genuineness could not be overshadowed by the petty jealousies of adolescence. She graduated in the top fifth of her class and pursued a career in nursing. Her romance with John faded gently into a warm memory for them both as they agreed to move on with their lives.

While in nursing school she began dating one of the carpenters employed by Matson Builders, and they were married shortly after her twenty-second birthday. The couple lived less than a quarter mile from Mel and Rita and eventually had three sons who brought boundless joy and happiness to their grandparents.

Dickie joined the Navy after high school, initially for the thrill of seeing the world, but he found his knack as a jet engine mechanic based in Norfolk. Whenever his ship visited a new country, he sent home a souvenir plate, which Rita displayed on what became known as "Dickie's Wall."

Probably the biggest surprise of the move was how Mel adjusted. From the time the family's station wagon pulled out of their driveway at the Beach, Mel never showed a hint of regret. It was if he was reborn by the move. His true spirit and personality came out as a salesman for Matson Builders, quickly learning the trade and gaining a keen sense of the business side of things. Tom Matson was a good judge of people and he knew that he had a gem in Mel. The two of them established themselves as a great team in the Raleigh housing market. Tom handled land procurement and subdivision layout while Mel coordinated marketing and sales strategy. After a few years, Tom proposed the company name be changed to "Matson-Rosco Development," but Mel declined. As he said, "Tom, everyone knows we're a team. I don't need to see my name up in lights to prove it."

Donny was fortunate to fall into an instant network of friends by rekindling his relationship with young Tommy Matson. Tommy introduced him to all his buddies. Beginning his sophomore year at a new school, Donny didn't make the same impact as Sylvia did. Her beauty, charm and grace radiated all around her wherever she was. Donny, on the other hand, kept a lower profile. But when he tried out for the school's cross-country team, he stunned himself and his family with his running ability. He had never considered himself much of an athlete but at Tommy's urging he gave running a try. Within a month he was keeping up with his best friend who had been a serious runner since eighth grade. By the end of the season, Donny had surpassed Tommy's best times and was the third fastest runner on the team. The entire family reveled in his success and no one was prouder of him than his friend Tommy. "I've created a monster!" Tommy would joke when talking of his friend's success. The Matsons and Roscos traveled all over central North Carolina for cross-country and track meets. They tailgated before and after the races. When the team competed at the state championships at N.C. State, it was the first time any member of the Rosco family had ever set foot on a college campus. The power of first impressions made its mark on Donny. He turned down several scholarship offers to run at smaller schools and decided to attend State. Mel and Rita were a little disappointed because this would signal the end of his competitive running career. They relished the excitement and atmosphere of the races but understood when Donny told them that he just didn't want to do it anymore. He would continue to be a dedicated runner, but now at his own pace.

During his freshman year at State, he became fascinated by the emerging field of computer science and chose that as his major. Donny achieved terrific grades and was offered an internship during the summer before his senior year. The upstart company was named In-tech, located in Tampa, Florida. The small software firm was looking for young, energetic people and Donny took a job with them after graduation.

Life was good for the North Carolina Roscos. The move seemed to have introduced everyone to a new way of life. Unfortunately, the future didn't pan out as brightly for Jimmy, Diane, and Freddy.

The Shack fire became a distant memory for the community, but it seemed to ignite more problems for Jimmy and Diane. After years of denial, they were finally forced into dealing with the behavior of their troubled son. The weight of covering up Freddy's crime caused an unbearable strain on the family and when a school counselor suggested they look into sending their son to a military school they both welcomed the idea. After lengthy talks with Freddy, all agreed that it was the best thing to do.

Freddy enrolled at a military school in Rhode Island and completed his entire high school years there. Upon his return to the Beach he was a more disciplined and considerate person, but in many ways a stranger to his parents. It came as a big surprise when he announced he wasn't interested in college, but instead, wanted to be involved with the family's business.

The regimentation and self-discipline Freddy learned at military school allowed him to turn his energies to more positive undertakings. He became devoted to learning all aspects of running the Shoreline Inn and within a few years he was capable of overseeing the whole operation himself. During the winter months, Jimmy and Diane spent extended time in their Florida condo while Freddy maintained the house at Woodland Beach. He had a couple of short romantic interests, but decided there wasn't enough room in his life to share with another person. By the late 1970s, Freddy had in effect taken over the family home and the responsibility of running the Shoreline.

When the economic downturn of the early '80s hit the area, merchants at the Beach immediately felt the pain. Jobs left the area by the hundreds as factories moved south or overseas, seeking cheaper labor. The days when a high school dropout was able to get a good-paying job in manufacturing were a thing of the past. Money became tight, people cut back on their outings to the Beach, and Jimmy's Shoreline Inn suffered. "For Sale" signs popped up all over town and the area continued to sink.

"Just one night's stay with us, Mr. Rosco?" the hotel clerk asked.

"Yes, just one night. I'll be flying back to Tampa tomorrow afternoon," Donny replied. The girl was an intern from the School of Hotel Management at Cornell and was home in Syracuse for the summer. She was determined to thoroughly cover every detail of Donny's check-in: restaurant schedules, shuttle service to the airport, happy hour at the bar. She continued on until Donny graciously thanked her and made up a white lie about having to make an important call. He was anxious to get settled in and drive his rental car to the Beach.

Donny made some calls to confirm his meetings the next day at Emerald Industries. The worldwide air conditioner manufacturer had been founded and was still headquartered in Syracuse. It remained one of the few shining stars in the area's sagging economy. Donny was here to pitch a new computerized payroll and inventory system that most businesses were adapting. The deal had huge potential for In-Tech and if his bid were accepted it would be the most lucrative contract in the young company's history.

Donny skipped the Thruway and drove the back roads to the Beach. Along State Route 31, what impressed him right away was the tattered and rundown appearance of everything. He'd read a few articles about the economic decline of the northeast, but this was the first time he had witnessed it for himself. Collapsing barns, houses that needed paint, abandoned cars in the grass — this wasn't what he remembered as a kid.

When he passed through South Bay, the lake came into view and the familiar sight lifted his mood. The white-capped waters, tall trees, and grandeur of it all, surprisingly, made him feel good to be back. Donny reached down to put some music on the radio and heard the whoop-whoop of a police siren behind him. When he saw the red and blue flashing lights his happiness sank.

He steered the car on to the shoulder, found the rental contract, and fumbled for his driver's license. *Damn! I don't need to have this happen to me right now*, he thought. A burly state trooper quietly appeared at the window.

"License and registration please, sir."

"How fast was I going, officer?"

"How fast do you think you were going?" the trooper countered. Donny handed over the documents and the trooper began writing on his clipboard.

"I don't know for sure — sixty, sixty-five maybe? I'm here on business and—"

"Donny? Donny Rosco?" the officer asked. Donny looked up and saw the brass nametag that read "C. Wilcox." When the trooper removed his dark glasses the pale face and blond hair confirmed it: Donny had been pulled over for speeding by the king of speeders himself, Carl Wilcox.

"Whoa! What on earth are you doing here, man?" Carl asked. Seventeen years of life seemed to melt away as, strangely, the two friends found themselves reunited along the side of the highway.

"Carl, when did you become a cop? I thought you were an auto mechanic."

"Been on the force about ten years now. I got hired to work on the cruisers and did that for quite a while, but in my spare time I took some courses at the community college. When Headquarters posted job openings for new troopers I gave it a shot."

Without the name tag, Donny wouldn't have recognized his friend from the old days at the Shack. Carl had always been an unassuming, scrawny looking teenager. Now, amazingly, he really filled out his uniform shirt: the guy was ripped!

"You look great. Did you start working out or something?"

Carl laughed and nodded. "Yeah, during basic training the other rookies introduced me to the weight room. They told me no one wanted to be seen hanging around a 'skinny dick-weed,' so here I am, thirty pounds and two shirt sizes later."

Some scratchy chatter came across Carl's hand radio. He pulled it from his belt, rattled back some police jargon, of which the only words Donny understood were ". . . Route 31 in South Bay."

Donny went on to explain his business trip and that he was driving to Woodland Beach to check up on the place. Carl asked about the whole family and was especially interested in how Sylvia was doing.

"You know Donny, I can tell you this now, but I really had the hots for your sister growing up."

"Yeah, who didn't back then? Our phone was always ringing off the hook for her." The two grown men shared a laugh.

"What do you hear from Ron and Ollie?" Donny asked.

"Well, I bump into Ollie all the time. He took over his old man's plumbing business and I see their truck driving around the area. He and his dad still get out on the lake to fish together whenever they can."

"I heard Ron joined the Air Force. Is that true?" asked Donny.

"He didn't have much choice. After you guys moved, he started having some problems and couldn't hold a job. He got to drinking pretty heavy and was in and out of jail. You know his temper. He never could walk away from a good bar fight. Well, after about his fourth arrest, the judge was so pissed, he wanted to put him away for a couple years. I called in a few favors from

Barretti who worked on the judge to give Ron one last chance. The judge ordered Ron to get some treatment for his drinking and to either find a steady job or join the service."

"Wow, I never heard any of this," Donny said.

"Remember that honey from Utica that Ron went out with the night of the fire?"

"Yeah, I think so."

"Well, apparently she recognized his name in the newspaper's police report and decided to look him up. Ron said that without her help, he never would have made it. He's a sergeant in the Air Force now and they have four kids. Ron works as some sort of supply clerk for airplane parts. Says it's boring as hell but he likes the job security and he's still sober. Mom and I get a Christmas card from him and Loretta every year."

"What about you, Carl, where you living?"

"Ah, I moved back in with my mom a few years ago to help look after her. I was married to a girl you never knew for a few years but it didn't work out. No kids."

There was a sadness in Carl's voice and Donny didn't know how to respond. Before he could, the walkie-talkie squawked again. It sounded more urgent this time and Donny could tell his friend would have to get going. Carl handed back Donny his papers and closed the clipboard.

"Great seeing you again," he said, shaking Donny's hand. "Give my love to your family, will ya?"

"You got it. Hey, what about my ticket?"

Carl let out a big laugh and hopped in the patrol car. He pulled alongside and rolled down his window to speak. "It's never been the same since that summer, Donny, never been the same . . ."

Donny nodded in return as Carl flipped on the siren and laid a gigantic patch of rubber down the highway. When the smoke cleared, he was out of sight.

Donny Rosco's hopes of seeing the Beach as he remembered it were quickly grounded when he crossed the canal bridge. Sadly, the scene before him was only more decline. It was a warm afternoon in late June, perfect weather for Woodland Beach, but the place was nearly empty. Driving slowly down Main Street, he counted three cars in the Shoreline Inn's parking lot. What he'd heard was true: the Beach was a failing entity. The entire town had an unwashed look to it. The pungent smell of fried fish outside the Shoreline seemed about the same, but other than that, Donny felt he was passing through a strange ghost town. When he turned onto Park Avenue the melancholy persisted as he drove past the vacant lot where the Shack had stood. Gratefully, his mood lifted when he saw the Lakeshore Hotel, still open for business. At last he felt some excitement at being back home. Eager to reconnect with his past, he decided to look up Steve and his boys.

Steve Mills had stopped off in Raleigh on his way to Florida two years after the Roscos moved, but this would be Donny's first reunion with Willis and Laparco. The fact that so many years had passed never dawned on him as he entered the barroom. He was happy to find that he place looked familiar: same shiny glass-covered bar top, warped wooden floors, and tattered leather stools. A couple of fishermen sat at the bar, one pontificating about the advantages of using live bait over man-made lures while the other stared into his beer glass. Donny smiled a silent hello toward them and sat down.

"What'll you have?" asked the barkeep.

"How about a Genny?" replied Donny.

"You got it, pal" the bartender answered. Donny noted the name "Ed" embroidered over the tall, bearded man's shirt pocket.

"You don't look familiar. What brings you to the Beach?"

"Just here for some business in Syracuse. Thought I'd stop by the old stomping grounds for a while."

"Well, you got the old part right," Ed joked. He returned to the other end of the bar by the fishermen and stooped over to scrub some glasses in the sink. "This joint is about ready to crumble or burn down like that dump across the street did," he added, motioning with his eyes toward the vacant lot where the Shack had stood.

Donny felt a tinge of hurt from the man's comment, but said nothing as this stranger proceeded to tell him how lousy the season was shaping up, and how he wanted to bolt from the area as soon as he could. "Some place down south" was all Ed replied when Donny asked him where.

Ed went on to tell him that tips were bad and the crowds were going elsewhere nowadays. The Lakeshore had stopped having live music five years ago and now brought in a DJ on weekends. Donny listened patiently and sipped his drink. This was the first time he'd ever drank Genesee out of a glass instead of a milkshake cup. It tasted about the same.

In Tampa, everywhere around him showed the energy of growth and newness. His life was so full of adventure these days, he really hadn't given serious thought to how this return to the Beach might be a disappointment. Sadly, the fond memories he longed for were locked up somewhere and he couldn't find the key.

"Steve around?" Donny asked.

"Who?" Ed replied. He was busy stacking the freshly washed glassware on a shelf.

"Steve Mills, the manager. Isn't he here today?"

"Never heard of him," answered Ed. "That must go back a ways. I've been here seven years and never knew a Steve Mills."

"How about Willis or Laparco?" Donny countered.

"Laparco! You just hit pay dirt!" Ed said, shaking his index finger playfully at Donny. "He's back in the storeroom with Doris. Want me to get him for you?"

"OK if I just walk back myself? I know where it's at," Donny said. He drained his beer and stood up.

"Suit yourself," Ed said. He drew two more draughts for a young couple who'd just walked in.

Donny peeked into Steve's old office and then slipped into the storeroom. Inside, he saw the backsides of a man and woman unpacking supplies and arranging them neatly on chrome wire shelves.

"Laparco?" Donny said lightly. The man and woman stopped their work and turned in unison. Yup, it was Anthony Laparco. The extra weight and graying hair were different, but that ever-present grin was the same.

"It's me, Anthony, Donny Rosco."

Laparco stared back at him with a blank look. Finally his brain connected the dots and he spoke, "Oh my god, I don't believe it! Donny, what are you doing here?" he shouted. He grabbed Donny's hand with both of his and shook it enthusiastically. Both men laughed freely, the way two old friends do when reunited unexpectedly.

"Just here for business and wanted to come by and say hello," Donny said. His eyes found the lady standing next to Laparco. She looked confused and a little frightened.

"Hi, I'm Donny Rosco, an old friend of Anthony's." He took her small hand and shook it gently.

"I'm Doris Laparco," she said, now more at ease and smiling nervously. Donny noted the slowness in her speech and the thick-lensed glasses she was wearing. She spoke with the slight impediment of someone mildly retarded but eager to be heard and understood. Donny looked back to Laparco who beamed lovingly at Doris.

"Donny, this is my wife," he said, never taking his eyes off her. She returned his gaze with a huge, proud smile.

"Anthony, congratulations, I didn't know you were married," Donny said.

"Been married three years now. We both work for Johnnie Montero, here at the Beach in the summer and at his bowling alley the rest of the time. Isn't she beautiful, Donny?" The short, round-faced woman blushed and elbowed her husband softly. The three of them broke out in a chuckle.

Laparco and Doris set their work aside and joined Donny at a table in the bar. Ed waved to the group and smiled. He wasn't sure what all this was about, but he'd been a saloon guy long enough to know when to leave people alone to their conversation. Laparco launched into an excited recap of his life over the last seventeen years. Donny quietly took it all in. After the Shack fire, life had gone on about the same for him, Willis, and Steve. Montero kept him on full time at the Lakeshore during the summer while he and Willis shared a place close to the bowling alley in the off season. Steve retired to Florida and always sent a Christmas card, but hadn't been up north for over ten years.

When Laparco finally paused, Donny asked, "Where's Willis?"

Hearing those words, Laparco's body jerked forward slightly, as if somebody had bumped him from behind. The grin left his face and Doris lowered her eyes to the table.

"Wil . . . Wil . . . Willis died few years ago," he stammered. His face grew red as he struggled to hold his composure. "I was coming back from the grocery store one day and found him on the floor of our apartment. His asthma got him, Donny. He ran out of medicine and couldn't breathe good. I called the ambulance right away but they couldn't save him."

Donny had unconsciously grabbed Laparco's hand while hearing the tale. A pang fell over him that can only be felt when hearing the belated news of an old acquaintance passing. The Roscos' lives had taken such a wonderful turn after the move. They had all but forgotten their past at the Beach. Donny felt shame at not knowing of Willis's death.

"I'm sorry about Willis, Anthony," Donny offered, not knowing what else to say.

Laparco nodded. They spent the next half hour talking about Mel, Rita, Dickie, and Sylvia. Donny invited Laparco and his wife to come down south some time for a visit. He knew that these two simple souls would probably never travel much farther than the next county for the rest of their lives, but they were flattered and joked about lying in the Florida sun. They said their goodbyes and Laparco gave Donny a big hug.

Anthony's mind traveled back to how lonely he'd felt that day on the beachfront when Donny's dad had hugged him and said goodbye. It took him months to get back his spirit after Mel left, but now Doris was in his life and he'd never be alone again.

As Donny drove away, Laparco and Doris waved to him like a couple of kids. The love and affection in their eyes made Donny miss his own family. He returned their waves, never turning his eyes toward the weed-shrouded concrete slab that was once the Shack.

Chapter Thirty

Donny turned slowly back onto Main Street. Passing the Shoreline again he decided to pull in; it was hot and he could use a soft drink for the hour-long drive back to his hotel. When he entered the Shoreline, it felt like he had walked into a dimly lit basement. The once immaculate, bustling restaurant had all the warmness of an empty, dingy warehouse. Jimmy's white-clad wait staff was nowhere to be found. Instead, a mish-mash of teenagers and older women, dressed in whatever moved them, were lingering idly throughout the building. Despite it being the prime dinner hour, the place was deserted.

Donny sat himself at the counter and picked up a menu. As he rested his arms, he felt something sticky against his skin. A previous customer had spilled a hot fudge sundae and the mess was never cleaned up.

"What do you want?" asked the pimply-faced girl behind the counter. She chomped on her gum incessantly.

"Just a Coke, to go, please," Donny ordered.

"What size?" the girl asked. She shifted the gum chewing into high gear.

"Large, please."

The young girl rolled her eyes, shook her head, and pivoted away. She grabbed a paper cup, jammed it into the ice-maker and begrudgingly poured the drink. *Man, how things have changed!* Donny thought. This never would have happened in the old days. Jimmy had been a stickler for service and demanded that his employees always smile while saying "please" and "thank you."

Rita's post office friends had relayed the news how things were different at the Shoreline and now Donny saw it for himself. Competition became brutal between restaurants to grab whatever customers still came to the Beach. A new Italian place sprang up across the bridge and gradually sucked away traffic from the Shoreline. Additionally, Moe LaGriggio, who probably hadn't changed his menu or tablecloths in twenty years, saw a rise in business as Jimmy's continued to decline. In a quest to improve the bottom line, Jimmy cut back on portion size, quality, and service, guessing wrongly that his reputation would carry them through. The days of the Shoreline's monopoly were over. Mel had once told Donny an old saying in the business: you can't give away bad food. Well, Jimmy's food wasn't bad, but you can't fool the public for very long. Many diehards still made the familiar pilgrimage for the Shoreline's Friday fish fry, more for nostalgia's sake than anything else. The younger generation, however, shunned the place.

With profits down, Jimmy and Diane took shorter vacations to Florida. They sold the condo and instead of renting an ocean-front unit like before, they stayed off the beach along A1A. Disenchanted with the financial setbacks, nonetheless, Diane continued to make her daily treks to sunbathe. One day, alone as usual on the sand, a wealthy businessman from Philly gave her the eye. Diane turned on the charm and welcomed the old man's affection with an open heart. He was divorced and looking for companionship. She was bored, lonely, and ready for a change. After a month and a half of them meeting on the sly, Jimmy came back to the room one afternoon to find her things gone and a terse goodbye note. It was no surprise; the marriage had never been the same after the Shack fire. The secrecy that she, Jimmy, and Freddy harbored draped a cold shroud around their family and any happiness they'd known together was gone. When Freddy partnered up with Jimmy to run the Shoreline, the two men paid little, if any, attention to her. Diane's life at Woodland Beach became a cold, miserable prison.

As Jimmy had stood there in the hotel room reading her note, he actually felt relieved. "One less thing I have to deal with now," he said out loud as he wadded up the paper and tossed it into the trash can. The divorce was simple, Diane settling for twenty thousand cash and happy to depart the sad, joyless life hers had become. She never even came back to gather her belongings. Freddy and Jimmy packed up her stuff and shipped it to Philadelphia.

Donny collected his change, picked up his Coke, and walked out the Shoreline's side door. As he sipped the cold drink and rounded the corner toward his car, he never saw the man carrying a large box coming from the opposite direction.

"What the fuck!" shouted the tall, skinny guy as they collided. Paper cups and napkins scattered to the sidewalk as the cardboard box tumbled down. Donny instinctively apologized and started picking up the mess.

"Didn't even see you," Donny said, without looking up. His drink had spilled down the side of his pants, but he ignored it. After a few seconds he glanced up, anticipating some response, and saw the face of Freddy Rosco — now over six feet tall and a disciple of Weight Watchers. Freddy backed off, speechless.

Donny, equally stunned, jutted out his hand and said warmly, "Hey, Freddy, how are you?"

"What are you doing here?" Freddy asked warily. *He might have lost some weight,* Donny thought, *but he sure didn't lose his arrogance.* Donny went on to briefly describe his business trip and why he was at the Beach. Freddy couldn't maintain eye contact with him and when the conversation took an uncomfortable pause, Donny offered up, "Well, say hello to your dad for me." He forced a smile while walking away, still waiting for a response.

"Donny, I hope you and your family are well," Freddy finally said. His eyes drifted downward again. "I never told you how sorry I . . ." his voice trailed off and his gaze returned to the sidewalk.

"I know, Freddy, I know," said Donny. He turned and walked to his car. As he drove out of the lot he saw Freddy still standing there alone on the sidewalk. They made eye contact but neither waved nor made any expression toward each other. As he accelerated onto Main Street, Donny thanked the Lord he no longer lived here.

On the drive back to Syracuse, Donny Rosco realized that the place he had once called home would never be the same again in his mind. The Beach was a spot that would forever kindle fond memories of the Shack, Steve Mills and his "boys" and the other beach rats he had known. That's the way he chose to remember the place. He vowed to never allow anything to taint that happiness.

After Donny had finished college and moved to Tampa, Mel took him aside one day and explained the entire circumstances of the Shack fire. He told him that, initially, he had suspected Donny might have somehow misread whether the fryers were off that fateful night in 1966. He had planned to bring it up to his son the next day, until Laparco approached him about seeing

Freddy. At that point Mel decided to keep quiet to see where the investigation led on its own. Mel held the secret for all those years because he saw no benefit in burdening any of his children. The family was so happy in North Carolina, why muddy the waters, he reasoned. Telling Donny was different, though. His older son was intimately involved and had a right to know. Rita, Donny, and Mel kept the secret intact. Neither Sylvia nor Dickie ever learned the truth.

Donny's presentation to the directors at Emerald Industries went well and he left their offices sooner than planned. He had given it his best shot and felt good about In-tech's chances of winning the contract. Even if his bid came up short, he could embrace the fact that his boss had the confidence to send him alone to negotiate such an important deal. After returning the rental car he found a pay phone and called his company in Tampa.

"Mike Faber's office, may I help you?"

"Hi Tina, this is Don Roscoe. How you doing?"

"Oh, hi Don. I was hoping you'd call before you left. How did everything go today?" she asked.

"I think we've got a good chance. The directors said they would like to make their decision by mid-July and we're one of the three finalists for the contract."

"Wow, that's great," Tina said.

"I finished up a little early and wanted to change my reservation for an earlier flight. Mike asked me to check with him first if my schedule changed at all."

"Right," replied Tina. "Mike is in a meeting right now, but he wanted me to tell you that everyone is knocking off at noon tomorrow, and for you to go ahead and start the weekend today. He wants to meet with you first thing on Tuesday the fifth."

"Man, I forgot all about it being July Fourth weekend! I've been pushing myself so hard getting ready for this presentation, it totally slipped my mind," Donny said.

"Yes, and a nice long one at that with the Fourth being on a Monday."

"We use to call that 'Golden,'" Donny said.

"What was that?"

Donny laughed. "I'll explain it over a beer someday, Tina, but where I grew up we called it a Golden Weekend when July Fourth fell on a Monday. It's a long story."

"OK. I'll take you up on that drink offer. Does this go against company policy if we're seen out together in public?" she teased.

"I hope not, because I've been wanting to ask you out for a couple of months, but haven't mustered up the courage," Donny admitted. He was embarrassed now.

"Well, I accept your invitation, Don. Let's talk about it when you get back," she said.

"I can't wait," Donny answered. He'd had a crush on the young redhead from Chicago ever since she came onboard as his boss' secretary last fall. He knew that she was single, but exactly how available, he wasn't quite sure. Things were really shaping up for him today.

"Tina, please let Mike know that since I'm not needed tomorrow, I'd like to change my plans and delay the connection out of Charlotte until after the weekend. I'll rent a car on my own and drive up to see my folks in Raleigh. Mike has their number if he needs me between now and Tuesday."

"I'll pass on the message. Enjoy the time with your family."

"Thanks, I will. Have a nice weekend," Donny said. He hung up the phone and smiled. He'd thought about asking Tina out a couple of times but always chickened out. Now, without even trying, he had a date. It was a miracle.

As he stood in line to board the plane, Donny retraced the last twenty-four hours. His return to the Beach had brought an awareness of how fragile and unpredictable life could be. He couldn't believe seeing Carl Wilcox behind the wheel of a cop car or hearing that Ron was a family man and Air Force lifer. Willis was gone, but Laparco had found Doris and the two of them seemed so happy.

The only family he had left at the Beach was Jimmy and Freddy, and he felt only pity for them. It seemed that the harder they pursued success and happiness, the further away those elusive goals drifted from their grasp. When his own family was at its lowest point years earlier, their faith and friendships were the only things they had to light the path. Mel and Rita struggled early on, but they never gave up.

Without even realizing it, they'd imparted two important life lessons to their children: first, always take the time to enjoy the good and simple things in life, and secondly, do your best to show loyalty and respect to the people you love, especially those who are the most vulnerable. If you did, good graces would come back to you a hundredfold.

Donny closed his eyes as the 737 lifted off the runway. His spirits soared right along with the jet. He was on his way home to see the people he loved. It truly was a golden weekend.

About the Author

Larry Carello was born and raised in Central New York State. During his career he has spent time as a short-order cook, construction worker, naval aviator and commercial pilot. He lives with his wife, Connie, in Michigan.